True Stories of 81 WEIRD HUMANS

PUSTAK MAHAL®

Publishers
Pustak Mahal®

J-3/16 , Daryaganj, New Delhi-110002
☎ 23276539, 23272783, 23272784 • *Fax:* 011-23260518
E-mail: info@pustakmahal.com • *Website:* www.pustakmahal.com

Sales Centre

- 10-B, Netaji Subhash Marg, Daryaganj, New Delhi-110002
☎ 23268292, 23268293, 23279900 • *Fax:* 011-23280567
E-mail: rapidexdelhi@indiatimes.com
- 6686, Khari Baoli, Delhi-110006
☎ 23944314, 23911979

Branches

Bengaluru: ☎ 080-22234025 • *Telefax:* 080-22240209
E-mail: pustak@airtelmail.in • pustak@sancharnet.in
Mumbai: ☎ 022-22010941, 022-22053387
E-mail: rapidex@bom5.vsnl.net.in
Patna: ☎ 0612-3294193 • *Telefax:* 0612-2302719
E-mail: rapidexptn@rediffmail.com
Hyderabad: *Telefax:* 040-24737290
E-mail: pustakmahalhyd@yahoo.co.in

ISBN 978-81-223-1270-6

Edition: 2012

Printed at : Param Offsetters, Okhla, New Delhi-110020

Contents

SIDONIA DE BARCSY

– The Bearded Baroness

Unlike many of her bearded lady contemporaries, the Baroness Sidonia de Barcsy was a genuine member of a royal family. Sidonia was born whisker-free on May 1, 1866 in Hungary. She remained sans mane until she gave birth to her son at the age of 19. Her son, Nicu, was a dwarf and was destined to stand less than three feet in height. The Baroness, meanwhile, began to sprout facial hair and in a few short months, Sidonia possessed a full beard measuring nearly 9 inches in length.

Sidonia's husband, Baron Antonio de Barcsy, was quite fond of the bushy beard. He took great pride in the unique appearance of his beloved wife and he relished the celebrity status she drew to the family. The Baron knew there was a fortune and actively cultivated a career for Sidonia and his son in exhibition and sideshow. In the pursuit of fortune and fame, the Baron moved his family to Western Europe in the the 1890's and the 'De Barcsy Troupe' began to actively tour to great success. The Troupe was certainly unique as it completely consisted of royal family members and was self-contained. With a blue-blood Bearded Lady as well as a dwarf on display, the Baron himself rounded out the troupe. At a weight of nearly 400 pounds, the Baron made for a rather respectable Fat Man and he displayed himself as such.

In 1903, the troupe travelled to America and found even greater fame than the Ringling Bros. and Campbell Bros. circuses. In 1912, while wintering in Oklahoma, the Baron became stricken with illness and passed away. Sidonia continued touring America until she died on October 19, 1925 due to complications associated with diabetes. Despite having remarried, Sidonia asked that her ashes be laid to rest next to the Baron.

The last member of the family, Nicu, continued to exhibit himself and perform in America. Adopting the title of 'Baron' following the death of his father. Baron Nicu was perhaps best known for performing at Coney Island as a magician and escape artist. Ironically, having lost the title to his family estate in a fire, Nicu was never able to return to Hungary to claim his royal title officially.

Nicu eventually retired in Enid, Oklahoma in 1932. There he was well-known and liked by the locals for his card tricks, his doves and his faithful dog. Nicu passed away in August of 1976 at the age of 91, the last member of a most remarkable family.

ANNIE JONES

– The Esau Woman

Shortly after she was born in Virginia on July 14, 1865, the hirsute Annie Jones began her career in exhibition. Purportedly born with a chin covered with fine hair, Annie's average parents were horrified by her appearance. It wasn't long, however, before the monetary benefits of their prodigious daughter dawn on the Jones family and word of her unique appearance came to the attention of elite showman P. T. Barnum.

When she was little more than a year in age, Annie was brought to New York City to be featured in Barnum's museum as 'The Infant Esau'. The name 'Esau' was often applied to hirsute wonders and was in reference to the biblical grandson of Abraham, brother of Jacob. Esau's name in Hebrew means 'hairy' and, according to Genesis 25:25, it is a reference to his hairiness at birth.

After an initial short but highly successful run, Barnum offered Annie's mother a three year contract, allotting Annie a weekly salary of $150 a week. Mrs. Jones accepted the offer which was exorbitant for the era, and took up permanent residence with her daughter in New York. However, within the first year of the contract, a family emergency called Mrs. Jones back to Virginia and she left Annie in the care of a Barnum appointed Nanny. During this time, Annie was kidnapped by a local phrenologist who attempted to exhibit Anne privately. Luckily, Annie was soon located in upstate New York, the kidnapper dealt with and Annie was quickly back in the custody of Mrs. Jones – who forevermore stayed in close proximity to her daughter during her career. Annie's career spanned thirty-six years.

During her long career, Jones travelled not only with Barnum's Greatest Show on Earth, but also worked in numerous dime museums. Annie's stage name changed to reflect her age during her career. She was known as the Esau Child and later as the Esau Lady and visually not only did Annie sport a full and long beard, she also grew out the hair on her head to over six feet in length. Annie also expanded her talents as well, as she was not content to simply be stared at. She came to be known for her musical skills and gracious etiquette as much as her facial hair.

At sixteen, Jones married Richard Elliot – a professional sideshow bally talker. The couple divorced after fifteen years. Jones then married another talker, William Donovan. Together, the newlyweds struck out on their own and toured Europe with Annie as an independent feature attraction and William as a vocal agent. Unfortunately, the marriage was short as William died without warning. Annie, not knowing what else to do, quickly rejoined Barnum's Greatest Show on Earth.

In 1902, Annie fell ill while visiting her mother in Brooklyn and on October 22, she passed away at age thirty-seven. Annie Jones was the most celebrated Bearded Lady of her era.

JEAN CAROLL

– Love Hurts

In her time, Jean Carroll was a popular bearded lady. More importantly, Carroll was the real deal. Born in 1910 in Schenectady, New York, Jean Carroll possessed the genuine foundation of a fine silken beard at the age of ten when she joined the Hagenbeck-Wallace Circus. As she aged, that foundation of follicles flourished and soon provided Carroll with a stable career in carnival exhibition.

As a young lady, Carroll met a charming young Ohio man and quickly fell in love. The object of her affection was John Carson. Carson was a charming and handsome man. He was a contortionist and sideshow talker and he was actually quite taken by the sweet-hearted bearded girl. He was certainly attracted to Carroll but the beard was simply too much for him to overcome. While he continued to be friendly with Carroll, he pushed aside any romantic aspirations and focused on friendship.

For fifteen years, the two saw each other almost daily. As Carson got to know Carroll as the woman she was, behind the whiskers, he fell deeply in love with her. Carroll saw that love in him and it pained her. She knew he would never be able to accept the beard and she, in turn, could not give up her source of livelihood and her home in the carnival. As she cried one night, sword swallower Alec Linton suggested a painful solution – "Shave the beard and become a tattooed woman."

Soon, the beard was gone and in its place were over 700 intricate designs by famed tattooist Charlie Wagner. The pain involved in the process was likely excruciating but the investment was wise. John Carson was completely smitten, apparently having no problems with illustration over facial hair, and the two wed almost immediately following the 'close shave'.

They remained with the carnival. John continued on in his old job as a charming sideshow talker and Jean Carroll exhibited her new tattoos quite thoroughly, as a burlesque dancer. The two remained inseparable until John passed away in 1951.

PERCILLA
– The Monkey Girl

The case of Julia Pastrana has long been held as a tragic example of exploitation. The remarkable bearded prodigy lived a life of manipulation and after death her body was abused and disgraced by callous souls and ignorance. The life of her contemporary could have easily followed the same shadowed path, however her story is of true love, inner beauty and respect.

During her long life, Percilla Lauther was known by many names. Originally, she was descriptively dubbed 'the hairy little girl' and later as 'the monkey girl', but it is quite likely that she will forever be remembered by those dear to her as Percilla Bejano – loving wife of Emmitt, the Alligator-Skinned Man.

The hirsute Percilla was born on April 26 of 1911 in the Puerto Rican town of Bayamon. Percilla had been born with hypertrichosis, she possessed two rows of teeth and drew immediate attention from the public and the medical community. Percilla's father was a native of Spain and he did not know what to do of his hairy daughter initially. Percilla's parents travelled to New York City seeking answers from American doctors and there they remained there for seven months until Percilla's father developed the idea of exhibiting his daughter for profit.

Percilla's father was not a greedy man. He merely saw an opportunity to make the most of the situation nature had thrust upon his daughter. However his limited knowledge of English and business made promoting Percilla difficult and he approached showman Karl. L. Lauther for assistance. Lauther was an accomplished promoter and he owned and operated several shows during his lifetime. He took an instant interest in Percilla and hired her on the spot. Lauther also hired an assistant to help Percilla's father care for the child after his wife returned to Puerto Rico. That arrangement was short lived however, as Percilla's father was shot and killed in Gainesville. Upon his death, and according to his final wish, Lauther adopted young Percilla as his own daughter.

Percilla never said anything ill of her adoptive father, thus one may assume that he was a compassionate and loving man. In fact, all evidence indicates that despite exhibiting Percilla for profit, Lauther was extremely sensitive to the public perception of his adoptive daughter. Lauther disliked the fact that the public took to calling Percilla a 'monkey girl' and verbally lashed out at anyone bold enough to call her a 'freak'. But the 'monkey girl' moniker stuck and Lauther gave in and began to publicly pair Percilla with a trained chimpanzee named Josephine. He may have had the last laugh, however, as the two attractions were juxtaposed. Percilla would warmly and graciously welcome guests to her exhibit while Josephine would rudely smoke cigarettes and spit.

In the late 1930′s, while performing with the Johnny J. Jones Exposition, Percilla met fellow marvel Emmitt Bejano, the Alligator-Skinned Man. Despite her heavy beard and his ichthyosis, a sweet romance blossomed between the unique couple. The pair saw past their physical differences. Emmitt was a man with calloused skin who spent performance intermissions submerged in vats of ice water because he could not sweat. Emmitt was quite literally 'thick skinned' and he had a 'hard shell to crack' but beneath he was a compassionate, gentle, charming and passionate man. Percilla, despite looking more beast than beauty, was elegant, eloquent and possessed an enchanting singing voice. Before long Percilla realised that the gentle Emmitt was the love of her life and the two eloped in 1938.

A year later, the couple welcomed a daughter, Francine, into their family. Unfortunately, pneumonia extinguished her life after a scant four months.

When Emmitt and Percilla returned to exhibition, they were promoted as the World's Strangest Married Couple. Percilla and Emmitt shared the stage and most notably worked for Ringling Brothers and other shows successfully for over a decade. They appeared together in the 1980 film Carny opposite Jodie Foster and Gary Busey. Eventually, the couple grew tired of life in the public eye, opted to retire to a private life in Gibsonton, Florida. There the two remained madly in love for many more years. Their union ended with Emmitt's passing in 1995.

Percilla carried on, clean shaven for the first time in her life, and briefly appeared in various documentaries and on the Jerry Springer show where she charmed the audience with stories of her beloved Emmitt and by shyly singing his favourite song 'It's a Long Way to Tipperary'. Percilla herself passed away in her sleep in February of 2001. She is dearly missed by all who knew her.

••

JULIA PASTRANA

– The Nondescript

The prodigious Julia Pastrana was known by many monikers during her life and perhaps just as many names in death. Both her life and her death are rather sad tales, but they hold a very special place in sideshow history because, for a time, she was not considered a member of the human race.

Julia's origins are shrouded in mystery. It is believed that she was born in 1834 to a tribe of 'Root Digger' Indians in the western slopes of Mexico. However, what is highly obvious is that Julia had appearance unlike any before her on record. In addition to excessive hair over her body – predominately in the face – Julia also possessed a jutting jaw and swollen gums. In odd juxtaposition to her ape like features, Julia possessed great poise, and a well developed buxom and a half foot figure.

Her documented career began in 1854 as she was exhibited in New York at the Gothic Hall on Broadway as 'The Marvellous Hybrid or Bear Woman'. Her 'handler' was one M. Rates who allegedly discovered the young Julia as a servant girl to the governor of Sinaloa, Mexico. While in New York, Julia attracted the attention of many scientific minds and media moguls. One newspaper described her as 'terrifically hideous' and possessing a 'harmonious voice', which gives evidence that she sang during her exhibition. Onc of the members of Medical society to examine her was Dr. Alexander Mott who declared her the most extraordinary beings of the present day and a hybrid between human and orangutan.

Julia then moved on to Cleveland with a new promoter J. W. Beach, and it was there that Dr. S. Brainerd declared her a 'distinct species'. That analysis was, of course, quickly added to all subsequent promotional materials.

Julia impressed many with her charm and grace. When invited to attend a military gala, she waltzed with many of the braver men there and, while in Boston billed as the Hybrid Indian: The Misnomered Bear Woman, Julia again impressed with her grace and singing voice so much so that she was put on exhibition by both the Horticultural Society and the Boston History Society.

Julia was preceded in London, England by impressive newspaper announcements touting her as 'a Grand and Novel Attraction'. And going by the epithet 'The Nondescript' – a term that in this era mean something unexplainable – Julia was now being shown by one Mr. Theodore Lent and was a rousing success. In fact, the bulk of the documentation on Julia comes from this time period, when London reporter could not stop debating her origins and describing her appearance in lengthy articles. In these articles, Julia is described as being very civilised and domestic. In addition to her native language, she also spoke Spanish and English quite well. She loved to travel, cook and sew. She willingly gave herself to medical examination and was said to have thirst for knowledge. These articles also seemed to emphasise that she was both happy and content with her situation and she did not covet wealth though her 'handler' Mr. Lent surely did. During her performances in London, Julia sang romances in both Spanish and English and danced what are described as 'fancy dances', likely traditional Spanish numbers.

After London, Mr. Lent secured a tour of Berlin and in Leipzig, Julia played the leading role in a play called Der curierte Meyer. In the play, a young German boy falls in love with a woman who always wears a veil. When the young man was not on stage, Julia would lift her veil to the great amusement of the audience. The play ends with the young man finally seeing his beloved and being cured of his infatuation. Following the play, the weekly magazine *Gartenlaube* published an extensive interview with Julia – an article published with a fantastic life sketch by the artist H. Konig. The article consisted of Julia speaking on her tours of America and London and of the numerous marriage proposals she had received. She claimed to have turned down over twenty admirers because they were not rich enough. That was a response that the reporter suspected Mr. Lent had coached – in the hope of attracting a rich suitor.

That notion was short lived and Mr. Lent, wary of loosing his investment in Julia to rivals, married her in 1857. While there was evidence that Julia was infatuated with her husband, Mr. Lent was not a kind man. While in Vienna, he forced Julia to undergo sensitive physical examinations and barred her from leaving their apartment during daylight. As their tour through Poland and Moscow continued, Mr. Lent became more and more controlling. In late 1859, while in Moscow, it was discovered that Julia was pregnant. The doctors feared a difficult childbirth due to Julia's stature and narrow hips; however Julia was more concerned that the baby should take after its father. On March 20, 1860 her fears were confirmed when she gave birth to a hair covered newborn boy. The child lived only thirty-five hours. And Julia died five days later.

During her lifetime Julia, though treated little more than an object by her promoters, did meet many influential people. She was visited by P.T. Barnum himself and even Charles Darwin acknowledged her in his book *The Variation of Animal and Plants under Domestication* with the words – 'Julia Pastrana, a Spanish dancer, was a remarkably fine woman. She had a thick and masculine beard.' Her condition at the time was unknown, yet given all the evidence: excessive hair, melodic voice, dental deformations and a child born with excessive hair – it was likely that she suffered from a form of hypertrichosis lanuginosa. All of her interviews and personal anecdotes promote the idea that she was a happy and content woman pleased with her lot in life. Yet, one is left with a sour feeling when reflecting on the events of her life. However, that is nothing compared to the feeling one suffers when recounting her afterlife.

Shortly after her death, Mr. Lent continued his commercial aspirations with Julia. He sold her corpse, as well as the body of his son, to Professor Sukolov of Moscow University. The Professor took the bodies to his Anatomical Institute, dissected them, and then using unknown embalming techniques mummified the bodies of Julia and her son. The entire process took six months and the results, while macabre, were impressive. Unlike the mummies of ancient Egypt, these mummified remains retained their colour, texture and form and appeared very lifelike. Sukolov placed the mummies in the anatomical museum of the University where they attracted great crowds.

When Mr. Lent heard of the profit his wife and child were earning after death, he went about legal proceedings to reclaim them. He presented his marriage certificate to the American consul and Sukolov was forced to release the remains. Lent tried to put the mummies on display in Russia but the authorities refused as they were outside the confines of a scientific institute. Thus, in February 1862, Lent returned to England to show Julia Pastrana again. The price was only a shilling and, with the added attraction of the mummified infant, the exhibit was packed with onlookers. Inside it was said that the 'Embalmed Nondescript' stood dressed in one of her many dancing costumes while her son stood to her left, atop a small pedestal and dressed in a sailor suit.

When the popularity of the exhibit began to fade, Lent rented the mummies to an English travelling museum of curiosities. In 1864, they were taken on a tour of Sweden. Most unbelievably, during that same time, Lent met a young lady with a condition very similar to Julia. In fact, unbelievably, the two looked so much alike that Lent married her as well and began touring her as Zenora Pastrana – Julia's sister. The mummy rejoined Lent for a time and the four of them toured together, however Lent rented the mummies to a Vienna museum and began to claim that Zenora and Julia were one and the same.

Lent and Zenora retired to St. Petersburg in the early 1880's and purchased a small waxworks museum. Lent was quite wealthy by the time, however he was unable to enjoy his wealth as, shortly after retirement, he experienced a mental breakdown and disappeared behind the walls of a sanitarium. It was assumed that he died shortly thereafter.

Zenora left Russia for Munich in 1888 where she reclaimed the mummies and toured with them – this time to prove that she was not Julia. In 1889, Zenora gave the mummies to an anthropological exhibit in Munich run by a man named J. B. Gassner before she retired again and remarried to a much younger man.

Gassner took the mummies to various German fairs and in 1895, he took them to a large circus convention in Vienna and sold them to the highest bidder. In the next twenty-five years, the mummies changed hands several times and showed up again in 1921 when a Mr. Lund bought them for his Norwegian 'chamber of horrors'. At this point, it is unclear if Lund knew these mummies were real as the medical community considered them lost.

In 1943, during the German occupation, the chamber of horrors collection was ordered to be destroyed, however Lund was able to convince authorities that a tour of the 'Apewoman' as Julia was called would prove beneficial to the treasury of the Third Reich. For several years, Julia and her son toured German occupied territories.

In 1953, Lund stored his chamber of horrors collection including the mummies in a large warehouse just outside of Oslo. For several years, rumours spread that the warehouse was occupied by a strange ape-like creature and one night in the mid 50's teens broke into the warehouse and Julia terrified them – some 80 years after her death. The experience and rumours that followed grew so popular that Lund's son Hans (Lund had since passed away) took the chamber out of storage and back on popular display until the mid 60's. Still, no one truly realised that these mummies were actual human beings.

That changed in 1969 when Judge Hofheinz, a very wealthy American collector of the unusual hired a small team of detectives to track down the mummies of Julia and her child. It was a circus director named Rhodin who eventually tracked down some pamphlets and posters and made contact with Hans. Aware of the priceless relic he possessed, Hans instigated a bidding war only to decline all offers and put the mummies back on exhibit himself. The press picked up the story of Julia and the exhibit proved so popular that it toured Sweden and Norway in 1970. In 1971, they made their way back to the United States – over one hundred years after the living Julia began her career there. The tour was cut short in America due to public outcry and when Hans attempted to return to Norway, he was denied exhibition rights. Undeterred, Hans rented the mummies to a Swedish travelling show until good taste arrived and the exhibition was banned there as well. Defeated, Hans placed the mummies in storage in 1973.

In August of 1976, the storage facility was broken and the mummies vandalised. The child was badly damaged as its jaw and arm were torn off. His remains were thrown in a ditch outside and before it could be located, it was almost entirely eaten by mice – only scraps remained. Julia then stood alone. In 1979, the storage facility was again broken and that time Julia was stolen. It was presumed that it too was destroyed.

Then in February of 1990, a Norwegian journalist discovered the mummy in the basement of the Institute of Forensic Medicine in Oslo. In 1979, police responded to a call involving some children who found an arm in a ditch. A search of the area revealed the mummified body of Julia, badly mangled. Unsure of what to do or even what it was, the police brought the mummy to the institute where it remained limbo – no one really paid any attention.

Apparently it is still there – tucked away in some corner covered with a dusty blanket.

••

MILLIE-CHRISTINE

– The Two-Headed Nightingale

Millie and Christine were born into slavery on July 11, 1851 in the town of Welches Creek, North Carolina. The girls were joined at the spine and their owner, a blacksmith named Jabez McKay, was not sure what to do with the girls. Their parents, Monimia and Jacob, had previously sired seven children but clearly the twins would be of little use to McKay due to their bizarre appearance and sickly constitution. Eventually, McKay opted to sell the eight-month-old girls and their mother to Carolinian showman John Pervis for $1000.

Pervis began exhibiting Millie and Christine immediately but within four years the girls were sold to showmen Joseph Pearson Smith and Brower and then kidnapped. The kidnappers exhibited the twins privately, mostly to members of the medical community for over three years while Smith and Brower frantically searched for their investment. They eventually located Millie and Christine while they were on exhibit in Birmingham, England. The law became involved in the situation and, as slavery was illegal in England, the girls were released into the custody of their mother. She, however, had no idea how to proceed with the girls in a foreign country and as a result she gave custody and ownership back to Smith.

While Smith continued to exhibit Mille and Christine, he found the public was not very interested. At the time, the anatomical novelty of conjoined twins simply was not enough to capture public attention. Smith decided to develop Millie and Christine as a performing act. Furthermore, he endeavoured to make the girls as extraordinary in skill as they were in appearance. To that end, he and his wife tutored the girls in music and languages. Millie and Christine were taught etiquette, social graces and were given music lessons. The girls developed impressive singing abilities and their singing prowess soon became the focal point of their careers. As 'The Two-Headed Nightingale' the conjoined girls started to gain a remarkable reputation. While Millie was a contralto and Christine a soprano, the girls were able to blend and harmonise their voices in incredibly appealing ways. By 1860, Millie and Christine were on the cusp of stardom.

In 1862 Smith died. The girls were willed to his son Joseph Jr. and it was Joseph who catapulted the girls to stardom by using a clever bit of showmanship.

Throughout their life, Millie and Christine were often considered one person. Due to their shared body, it was often unclear if the girls were legally and physically a single being or individuals. The girls themselves often referred to themselves in the singular, using 'I' in the place of 'we'. Joseph Jr. saw opportunity in this confusion and opted to advertise the girls from a new perspective. The girls became Millie-Christine, a girl with two heads, four arms and four legs.

The concept of such an incredible phenomenon drew immediate crowds and Millie-Christine enjoyed immediate and worldwide popularity. Furthermore, it was the singing of 'The Two-Headed Nightingale' that quickly gained predominance over appearance and Millie-Christine eventually performed for European royalty, including the Prince of Wales and Queen Victoria. Mille-Christine became renowned for singing, playing the guitar and piano in unison and dancing the waltz in front of thousands of people in the greatest halls and venues of the world. Soon, the Emancipation Proclamation came into effect and Millie-Christine was free. During the course of her career, Millie-Christine earned more than $250,000.

Millie-Christine preformed until the age of fifty-eight. Once retired, Millie-Christine became Millie and Christine once again. The sisters built a home in Columbus, North Carolina where they lived quietly till their death on October 8, 1912. Millie went first, succumbing to tuberculosis, and her sister followed seventeen hours later. They were sixty-one, the oldest conjoined twins on record.

07 ROSA & JOSEPHA BLAZEK

– The Bohemian Twins

The conjoined sisters Rosa and Josepha Blazek were born in Skrejsov, Bohemia on January 20, 1878. The two were pygopagus – joined at the posterior. They shared tissue and cartilage but were also joined at a thoracic vertebra. It was that delicate fusion that negated any possibility of separation and when their mother took them to Paris at the age of thirteen, doctors told her just that.

It was in Paris where the twins began their career in professional exhibition. Depending what story you believe, until that point their mother was either adamantly against displaying her daughters for profit or limited their publicity to local fairs. But the twins themselves saw Paris as an opportunity to get out of their tiny village. They found a manager, learned to sing and play the xylophone, and began drawing crowds.

Like many conjoined performers, much was made of their differences in personality and tastes. Rosa was considered the sharper of the two. She was witty and talkative while Josepha was introvert. Physically Rosa was the more dominant of the two sisters. Josepha was slightly more deformed than her sister, with her left leg being substantially shorter than her right. In matters of promotion, the pair was heavily sexualised and posters for their appearance at the Theatre Imperial de la Gaiete featured with bared midriffs and tight corsets. As a result the public conjectured on their sexual activity and the complications their physical condition posed.

The Blazek sisters were famous in the 1890's as they toured Europe. They eventually become quite skilled on the violin and stunned crowds with their enthusiastic duets. But, by the turn of the twentieth century, their popularity quickly evaporated due to poor management and overexposure. Their obscurity was shattered in 1909 when Rosa claimed to be pregnant. Controversy spread like wildfire and rekindled their celebrity.

To the public, the idea of such a liaison was bewildering. Although the twins had separate vaginae, their physical proximity seemingly made any tryst a ménage à trois. The newspapers filled with rumour laced articles. Some believed the twins were sex crazed harlots; others depicted Josepha as an unwilling victim. Rosa claimed she had intercourse only once and she refused to name the father. There was much speculation that their manager was the father and he paid the duo to keep quiet. Regardless of the paternity, on April 16 1910 'Little Franz' entered the picture.

As Franz grew, he joined the twins' travelling show as 'The Son of Two Mothers' and with their newfound celebrity the three of them left Europe and appeared in the united states, previously only visiting America during the 1893 Columbian Exposition in Chicago. The twins set their sights on vaudeville and established a base in Chicago but their dream of the American stage was cut short when Rosa fell ill with influenza. As Rosa recovered, Josepha became sick and her illness soon overcame her. Doctors were uncertain of the diagnosis and shortly after being admitted into Chicago's West End Hospital on March 22, 1922, Rosa fell into a coma.

A brother, Frank, appeared out of nowhere and once Rosa also succumbed to a coma, Frank spoke for the sisters. Newspapers disagree on the final days of the Blazek twins. Some claim Frank would not allow any attempt at surgical separation and others claimed Rosa was adamant about remaining joined or just as adamant about being separated. All newspapers agreed that Frank was a gold digger who only had his eye on their fortune.

Josepha Blazek died on March 30, 1922. Rosa followed her twelve minutes later. With their death, another media frenzy began around who was entitled to their fortune. Soon after they were laid to rest, the matter was a moot point. It was discovered that the pair only had a savings of $400 between them.

Even today, much controversy exists regarding the origins of Franz. Many historians and authors believe that the boy was nothing more than a well timed publicity stunt. While an autopsy confirmed that the two had separate uteri, it fails to mention any evidence of pregnancy. In fact, any evidence points to the contrary.

In addition, stories of the paternity of Franz changed during the time the boy toured. At one point it was claimed that the baby boy was named after his father, a soldier named Franz Dvorak. It was claimed that Rosa married the soldier shortly before his death in 1917. But there is no record of the marriage, nor did the man ever appear publicly with his family. It was likely a story engineered to evoke sympathy and further attendance.

It is known that Franz did spend time in an orphanage, and some believe that is where the boy originated from in the first place. The fate of Franz is currently unknown as he disappeared into history following the death of the Blazek twins.

••

RADICA & DOODICA

– The Indian Siamese Twins

The term 'Siamese twin' is synonymous with the medical condition of conjoined twins. This term is due to the mid 19th century popularity of Chang and Eng Bunker, joined twins who originally hailed from Siam. The brothers were so popular that their billing as Siamese twins came to represent their condition and not their nationality, even though the depth of their intermingled connectivity was not overly impressive compared to conjoined twins like the Tocci Brothers. The Bunker brothers were primarily joined at the chest by only a band of cartilage.

In 1888 in Orissa, India twin girls were born connected in a similar manner. While the birth of conjoined twins was often viewed as highly unusual, the superstitious residents of their village saw the girls as 'symbols of divine wrath' and lobbied for their expulsion. Their father, distraught by the appearance of his daughters, moved to physically separate the girls by his own hand but local officials rescued the infants and the monks of a local temple took over their care. The monks named the girls Radica and Doodica.

In 1893, Radica and Doodica were sold to London showman Captain Colman. The sisters began a career exhibiting themselves across Europe often paired with another Colman prodigy, a dwarf billed as the smallest man in the world, Peter the Small. It has been said that Colman treated the girls as an adoptive father and not exclusively as an exploitive promoter. The girls seemed happy and they had each other, until Doodica developed tuberculosis in 1902.

In Paris, Dr. Eugene-Louis Doyen separated the sisters in an effort to save Radica. Doyen was a pioneering medical filmmaker and filmed the twins' surgery as *La Separation de Doodica-Radica.*

The operation was considered a success initially and Doodica passed shortly afterward from tuberculosis. However, the separation came too late as Radica contracted tuberculosis from her sister and died in 1903. She spent the last year of her life in a Paris sanatorium, alone.

Sections of Doyen's separation surgery were last shown in the UK documentary series *The Last Machine* in 1995. Previously, the film was often shown in grindhouse styled sideshows spliced into exploitation 'freak' films.

••

09 THE TOCCI TWINS

– The Blended Brothers

Giacomo and Giovanni Batista Tocci are something of a strange enigma. Despite being enormously popular with both the public and the medical community during their career, little is actually know about the joined siblings. Furthermore, what is known is often confusing and contradicted by various sources.

What is certain is that the brothers were born in Locana, Italy. However sources cannot agree on the date of their birth. It is safe to assume that the boys were born in early October, 1877. Their mother was only 19 at the time of their birth, her first child (children). Since the boys were tiny, the birth was apparently an easy one. Reports indicate that the Tocci family welcomed a total of nine children, all average except the twins.

The only other thing certain about the brothers is that they were dicephalus twins joined at the sixth rib. Their abdomen consisted of separate hearts and organs and each of the brothers had two functional arms. However, the two were as one below the point of fusion and shared intestines, a pair of legs and one set of genitalia.

The brothers had great difficulty walking. Each brother controlled one leg and many believe they lacked the co-ordination required to walk. Again, some believe that this was not the reason for their difficulty as subsequent dicephalus twins have mastered bipedal walking. Giacomo had a clubfoot and many attribute this to their lack of mobility. Regardless of the reason, instead of walking, the brothers used their arms for locomotion. Their mode of transport was once described as 'spider-like'.

From birth the brothers were exhibited around Europe with their father as manager, which eventually led to a very influential tour of the United States in 1891. During their visit, author Mark Twain was so inspired by their appearance that he used them as the basis for his short story *Those Extraordinary Twins*. It was also in the United States that the brother adopted their most famous moniker, 'The Blended Brothers'. In 1892, the twins performed in New York and in a bit of showmanship their billing claimed that one boy spoke only German and the other only French. For the performance, which was preceded that evening by Jo-Jo 'The Dog-Faced Boy', they obliged. The brothers spoke several European languages.

Throughout their life, the twins were the subject of intense medical examination. Their first complete examination was performed one month after their birth. They first appeared in medical literature, Lyon Medical Magazine, following an 1878 examination in Paris. While touring Vienna in 1881, they were touted by the medical community as 'The Greatest Wonder in the World'. The twins were subject to illustration and photography, including a nude set.

The intelligence of the boys continues to be the subject of much debate as many articles refer to Giacomo being 'somewhat idiotic' when compared to his brother. However, those observations were made during infancy and later reports make no mention of any discernable intellectual deficiency. In fact, later reports hail Giacomo as being the more artistically creative of the two.

In 1897, at the age of 20, the boys decided to retire. Together, they had made a great fortune for themselves and their family. During their peak, they made more that $1000 a week. But the boys never really cared for the fame thrust upon them. They purchased a high walled villa near Venice. In 1904, the boys married two seperate women. It appeared in the media and caused a great controversy. The knowledge of their shared genitalia was public knowledge and their wives were labelled as vulgar.

••

THE HILTON SISTERS

–Chained for Life

Contrary to popular belief, outright exploitation was not very common in sideshow. The majority of human wonders displayed themselves for their own reasons and quite often reaped massive financial and personal rewards for doing so. However, of the few performers who were exploited against their will, the tale of Daisy and Violet Hilton ranks as one of the worst.

Daisy and Violet were conjoined twins born in Brighton, England on February 5, 1908. The sisters were born pygopagi, joined at the posterior. The sisters shared no internal organs and all that was truly uniting them was bone, muscle and skin.

Their birth name was Skinner, however their impoverished and unmarried mother, Kate could not fathom the responsibilities involved in raising a pair of girls joined. She sold the twins to her boss and midwife Mary Hilton. Williams instantly saw potential profit in the twins.

According to many sources, including the autobiography written by the Hilton sisters in 1942, Mary Hilton was a strict, physically abusive, exploitive and corrupt human being. The twins were 'trained' and 'groomed' to sing and dance in the vaudeville tradition. While this training was in progress, the horrific abuse and dehumanising continued. When the girls finally began touring, they were seen as little more than possessions by the Hiltons.

The twins proved to be hugely successful and the toured extensively beginning at the age of three. On stage, the pair looked like dolls, their blonde hair in curls and bows on their shoes. Violet played the piano while Daisy played the violin.

Billed as 'The United Twins', their tours of Germany, Australia and the USA often saw record crowds. The twin brought in enormous amounts of money. Mary Hilton kept every penny.

When Mary finally died in Birmingham, Alabama, the guardianship of the twins fell to Mary's daughter Edith and Edith's husband, Meyer Meyers. They were even worse than Mary as they controlled every movement the twins made. They also proved to be poor agents as they insisted on keeping the girls 'dolled up' as little girl well past the age it was acceptable. Critics took notice and the twins were allowed to grow up, but only a little.

The mistreatment and corruption continued under the dictatorship of Edith. Edith purchased a mansion in San Antonio with the money the twins earned. The twins spent much of the 1920's touring the United States on vaudeville circuits. It was on these circuits that they met Bob Hope and their dear friend Harry Houdini. Their popularity, at this point was near its peak and as a result they became subject to scandal.

The twins had befriended their advance agent, William Oliver. Oliver's wife Mildred was suspicious of the relationship and accused William of improper acts. A postcard from the twins signed to William 'with love' prompted Mildred to file for divorce and sue the twins for $250,000. Oddly enough, this frivolous lawsuit was the catalyst for the Hilton's freedom.

During a visit to San Antonio lawyer, Martin J. Arnold, the truth came out. As the Meyer's were out of the room, the Hilton sisters told the lawyer of their life of abuse and captivity. The lawyer was flabbergasted and immediately took on the twins' case. He took the twins into protective custody.

In April of 1931, Judge W.W. McCrory awarded a large sum of money – some reports say as much as $100,000 to the sisters and granted the pair their freedom. The girls had spent 21 years in abject slavery.

Daisy and Violet became citizens of the United States and returned to show business. They hosted their own show, 'The Hilton Sisters' Revue'.

Everything seemed to be perfect in the life of the Hilton sisters; however, the pair soon began to self destruct. Due to too many years of solitude, suppression and deprivation, the girl wallowed in excess. They had numerous affairs, legal problems, clashes with that media and a couple of short publicity marriages. Their popularity nosedived. In 1950, the sisters appeared in their final film 'Chained for Life'. It flopped and the pair further failed in an attempted food franchise. By the 1960's the pair were nearly penniless.

The Hiltons' last public appearance was at a drive-in movie theatre in Charlotte, North Carolina in 1962. Their tour manager abandoned them there, as the tour was a failure and he was tired of losing money. He left them without any money or transportation and the twins simply decided to settle in Charlotte. A kind grocery store manager hired the sisters to work in his shop, where they checked and bagged groceries.

On January 6, 1969, the twins failed to report for work and were found dead in their pious home. They had no surviving family.

Despite the sad end to their lives, the memory of the Hilton sisters still lives on. In 1997, a Broadway musical loosely based on the sisters' lives, Side Show, with lyrics by Bill Russell and music by Henry Krieger, received four Tony nominations.

RITTA & CHRISTINA

– Early Conjoined Twins

Ritta and Christina Parodi are likely the best documented case of conjoined twins in the early 19th century. The details of their life and death, in the form of detailed autopsy reports, are well-known. Their life was remarkably short, due in part to their popularity.

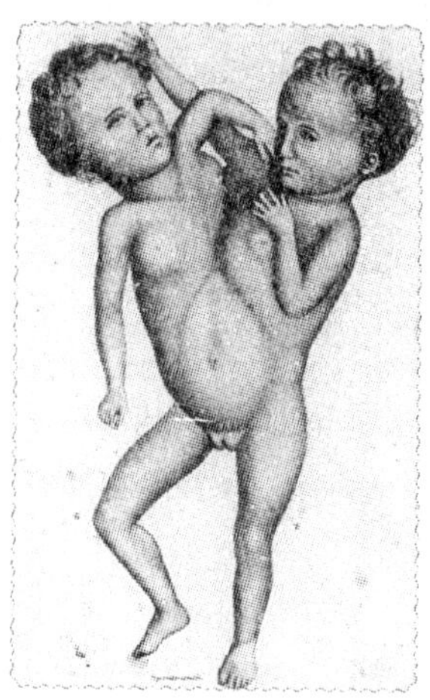

The twins were born in Sassare, Sardina on March 3, 1829 and were the last in a family of eight. The Parodis were quite poor, but upon the birth of the twins they spent their savings on a trip to France, with the assumption that doctors and naturalists would scramble to study the twins. However, upon arriving in France, the family had no idea of how to promote the twins and became increasingly destitute. They initially tried to display the twins publicly but were constantly denied by city officials. Eventually, word did get out and physicians came to them. Unfortunately, constant observation interrupted the twins sleep and exposed them to chills. Ritta, who was sickly since birth and steadily growing weaker, quietly passed on November 23, 1829 while suckling from their mother. Christina, who up to that point had been both healthy and alert, died only moments later. They had lived for only eight months.

The pair was distinct from the shoulders up. But below the navel they shared one set of genitals, one anus, on pelvis and onc sct of legs. During autopsy, it was revealed that the viscera of the pair were transposed to each other. The viscera – heart included – formed mirror images of each other. It was likely this 'backwards heart' that caused Ritta to be so sick and weakly. The twins' skeleton as well as a plaster cast of their body is currently in the possession of the Natural History Museum in Paris. However, neither is currently on display.

ELIZA & MARY

- The Biddenden Maids

One of the oldest professional conjoined twins to display themselves for livelihood were the Biddenden Maids. Eliza and Mary Chulkhurst were born in 1100 to an upper class family in just outside of Kent, England. The pair were likely pygopagus twins and most illustrations show them as such. There are a few anomalous images depicting the pair joined at the shoulders as well; however, this was likely due to an artists working from description only.

When one twin died in 1134, the remaining one refused separation, saying, "As we came together, we will also go together." She died just hours after her sister.

The twins were quite wealthy in life and left their fortune to the poor, a fortune that included 20 acres of land. The people of Biddenden were so enamoured with the sisters and their gracious gift that until the early 1900's an annual festival was celebrated in their honour. In a somewhat unusual tradition, the creation of 'Biddenden Cakes' – featuring depictions of the sisters – were common and a staple treat during the celebration.

While the festival is gone, a row of homes bearing the name Chulkhurst remain on the land the pair donated.

SAMUEL PARKS

– Hopp, the Frog Boy

The man who came to be known as Hopp, the Frog Boy, Samuel 'Sam' Parks, lived a life both cursed and charmed.

Sam was born on October 20, 1874 in Boston and his first public appearance was at the age of 19 and for the benefit of medical students at the 1893 Chicago World's Fair. Sam Parks was likely born with osteogenesis imperfecta – a condition that resulted in brittle bones and regular painful fractures. According to a souvenir pamphlet distributed by Parks in his 16th year of public display, he personally recalled breaking 58 bones during his lifetime. Parks likely broke many more in his youth. These multiple fracture resulted in a dwarfed, stunted and contorted body. His legs, in particular, were twisted and bowed and it was from his bowed legs that his moniker of 'The Frog Boy' originated.

Parks was from a poor family. His father worked hard to support the family. Sam learned to be independent as he did not want to be a burden to his family and he endeavored to push the limits of his fragile body. As a result Sam would still require care and assistance but he was a proud man who would try and fail before asking for help.

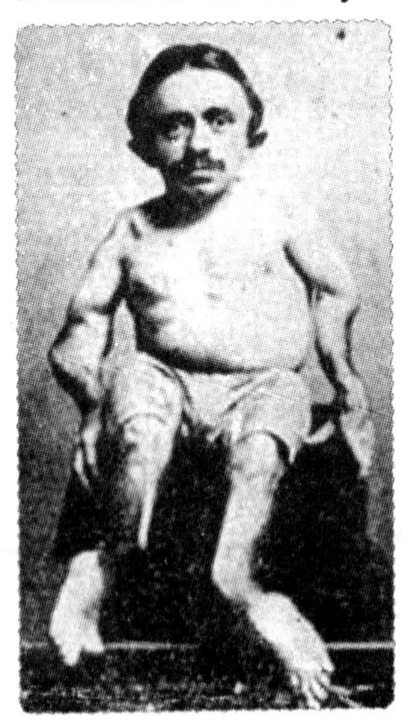

Shortly after his first public appearance, Sam Park began a full fledged career in human exhibition. Parks embellished his true origins, played on his amphibian appearance and as a human oddity he began to earn a good living appearing across the United States in carnivals and dime museums.

Remarkably, in 1906, Parks found love and married Maryland native Ida

Granville in Baltimore. However, his euphoria was cut short when less than a year later his manager absconded with all his personal financial fortune and left him penniless on tour in Georgia.

A year later, Parks had rebuilt his fortune and welcomed the birth of his first child, a healthy son. Sadly that happiness was also short-lived and, as Parks prepared to welcome his second child into the world a year later, he found himself mourning for his wife Ida. Both his wife and the infant died during childbirth.

Parks was devastated and his shattered heard mirrored his broken exterior. By 1909 Sam Parks was a widower with a young child to feed. Parks was a broken man inside and out. His health deteriorated and he found his mobility was becoming more and more difficult as his body continued to break beneath him. Parks prepared himself for a lifetime of lonely solitude as he knew his physical limitation would not allow him to care for his son and that a second chance at true love was unlikely.

In 1910, while touring Canada with Great Patterson Shows, Parks met a young dwarf in passing. The Austrian born little lady was charming and Sam found her adorable. As he did in childhood, Sam again refused to acknowledge his limitations and was determined to court the young lady. In that same year Sam Parks married Helen Himmel, the famous 'Princess Wee-Wee', and the two lovers were evermore billed together as 'The World's Strangest Couple'.

The couple continued to tour for a few more years. Sam eventually did welcome a second child, another son into his family as Helen gave birth in 1911. After retiring from exhibition, Sam worked at small newsstand in El Paso until his passing on October 23, 1923 at the age of 49.

Samuel Park experienced a life of great pain. But in his lifetime his heart felt the joy of true love a fair trade he paid with no complaints.

KOO KOO

– The Bird Girl

There are a handful of human wonders who seem to transcend time, culture and societal norms. These truly unique few become forever recognisable and iconic to the general public. Joseph Merrick, the Elephant Man will be forever famous due to his unforgettable visage. Likewise, Jo-Jo, the Dog Faced Boy will forever be famous for his shaggy face and Zip, the Pinhead will always furrow brows in faint recognition when his moniker is mentioned. These individuals captured the interest and imagination of the public and continued to be referenced in pop culture decades after their prime.

However, one strange character who managed to obtain this 'celebrity of strange' wasn't really that strange at all. Or, at least, not when compared to other more 'impressive' marvels saddled with physical limitations and socially crippling conditions.

Minnie Woolsey was born in Georgia in 1880 and a wide variety of stories exist in regards to her physical condition. It is generally believed that Minnie was born with Virchow-Seckel syndrome, a condition also known as bird-headed dwarfism. The syndrome is quite rare and is characterised by a small head, stunted growth, beak-like nose, receding jaw as well as some mental limitations. In addition, the syndrome also left Minnie almost completely bald and blind. Toothless, odd and sporting glasses as thick as her thumb, Minnie spent the majority of her formative years in a Georgia asylum until, as legend states, she was rescued by a showman who thought her oddball looks were just odd enough to cash in on.

Minnie began her sideshow career dressed in an American Indian costume and billed as 'Minnie-Ha-Ha'. The name was an obvious play on North Carolina's Minnihaha Falls and the gimmick was likely a nod to the Aztec Children exhibits of yesteryear. Minnie, initially reluctant and shy, soon came to love the attention she received as a sideshow attraction. She was known to dance and shake excitedly and to speak in thrilled gibberish to the delight of audiences everywhere.

In 1932, Minnie landed a role in Freaks as Koo Koo – the Bird Girl and a film legend was born. The image of Minnie, dressed in a feathery costume complete with tiny plumed cap and chicken-like feet, shimmying atop a table during a wedding feast is forever synonymous with the film. Once you see Minnie's performance, you will never forget it. In fact, there was actually another 'Bird Girl' in Freaks but few remember poor Betty Green as she was completely overshadowed by Minnie. Today Betty Greene is generally only remembered, in error, as being Koo Koo from Freaks.

Following her film debut, Minnie continued to perform as Koo Koo – the Bird Girl and continued to wear her strange little costume for a number of years. Eventually, she had stints at Coney Island where she was billed as 'The Blind Girl from Mars'. By that time, age or perhaps boredom had taken hold and the dancing had stopped. Minnie's 'Blind Girl' act consisted primarily of standing or sitting near comatose, deadpanning all audience jeers and interactions.

How long Minnie was involved in human exhibition and how she passed are something of a mystery. Some accounts state that she performed well in her 80's. There are also reports that Minnie was hit by a car in the 1960's. Regardless of how her life ended, her peculiar appearance ensured her a small level of immortality.

AL & JEANIE TOMAINI

– The Strangest Couple

Al (Aurelio) Tomaini was born in 1912 in New Jersey as one of seven children. By the age of twelve he towered over his father – a stout man who stood over six feet in height. Al had an overactive pituitary gland and he eventually stood over seven feet in height. To earn a career in sideshow, Al claimed a height of 8'4" and billed himself as 'The Tallest Man in the World'. No one seemed to mind Al's embellishment, due to the fact that Al was an incredibly genuine and nice guy. He was shy, gentle and sweet inside and out – from the top of his towering head to the bottom of his size 27 shoes. During the Great Lakes Exposition in 1936, one special young lady took a particular interest in the gentle giant with the coy smile.

Her name was Jeanie (Berniece Evelyn Smith) who was born on August 23rd in 1916 in Bluffton, Indiana with twisted arms and without legs. She 'stood' just over two feet in height but, in personality, Jeanie was a giant in her own right. Jeanie had been performing in exhibitions since the age of three and was known for her acrobatic dexterity and the nimble way she ran about on her mildly deformed hands. Originally exhibited by her biological mother, Jeanie had been under the abusive care of an adoptive mother since 1931. The pretty but resilient 19 year old endured the psychological abuse with little hope of escape but, when the sincere flames of romance sparked between her and Al Tomaini, she found a gargantuan protector who would forever lift her out of harm's way.

The unusual couple eloped during a fair in Cleveland, Ohio on September 8th of 1936 and were wedded by a justice of the peace the same day. The pair honeymooned in Niagara Falls and continued touring together for many decades as the 'World's Strangest Married Couple'. In the off season they settled in Gibsonton, Florida. It was there that the two remarkable people built a home and a life together.

Gibsonton was known for its population of unusual people. Many circus folk retired or wintered there and many still do. Al and Jeanie purchased a piece of property there along the banks of the river and established a lodge and fishing camp known as 'The Giant's Camp', marked by one of Al's enormous cowboy boots nailed to the nearest road sign. In Gibsonton, Al and Jeanine raised two adopted daughters. With their savings and camp earnings, the pair bought and donated an ambulance to their town. Al served as the world's tallest fire chef and president of the Chamber of Commerce. Al even lent a hand in building the community hall. All the while, the pair were inseparable and deeply in love. Al was often spotted with his pretty half-girl wife Jeanie propped on his shoulder or carried at his side.

Fortified by that love, Al lived longer than most pituitary giants. He likely endured much physical pain but refused to show it. Eventually, however, his time came and he left his beloved Jeanie in 1962 at the age of 50.

Jeanie continued without her giant husband. She never remarried and continued to run the camp until her own passing on August 10, 1999. She was buried on the anniversary of Al's passing.

The Tomaini family still reside in Gibsonton. Their great-grandson, Alex Zander Marrow, carries on their circus sideshow legacy by performing amazing feats of physical endurance professionally as the Junior Torture King. He was formerly the youngest sword swallower in the world and his grandmother, the Tomaini's adopted daughter Judy, built him his first bed of nails.

ROBERT HUDDLESTON

– The Pony Boy

For many years the world only knew Robert Huddleston as The Pony Boy and by the astounding images depicting his unusual posture. Following his years of travel with carnivals as a human exhibit, his true name and story were nearly lost to history and his story of personal triumph and perseverance has only recently resurfaced.

Like Ella Harper, The Camel Girl, Robert Huddleston was likely afflicted with a very advanced form of congenital genu recurvatum, also known as 'back knee deformity'. By most accounts, Robert was unable to stand erect or use crutches, so he lived and trekked about exclusively on all fours.

Despite what appeared to be a crippling affliction, Huddleston lived a remarkably active lifestyle and possesses a remarkable work ethic. Born around Excelsior Springs, Missouri in 1895, Robert Huddleston spent much of his childhood working chores on the family farm by milking cows, loading stock and harvesting crops. Huddleston spent his early adulthood employed as a logging teamster where he hauled trees and lumber some fifteen miles a day while affixed to a wagon. He protected his hands from rocks and bush debris by lashing small wooden blocks to his hands with leather and as a result of this heavy labour Huddleston's arm and shoulder strength practically became legendary among his peers. To punctuate his independence and mechanical inclination, Huddleston was employed as a blacksmith and as a carpenter temporarily during World War II.

To those who knew him, Robert was a kind hearted and hardworking man who ignored his perceived limitations. Most of them not even notice his physical condition as it was never an issue. Still, strangers stared and work became rather scarce following WWII and Huddleston soon considered exhibiting his physical appearance and extraordinary independence for profit.

Huddleston came to be known as 'The Pony Boy' following the war while showcasing his physical uniqueness for the first time in a small carnival located in Texas. The brief stint proved incredibly successful, likely due in part to his exceptional work ethic, and led to more work with several larger organisations. Eventually, Huddleston toured all of North American with the Tom Mix Circus. His act consisted primarily of displays of strength combined with unique flexibility. It's been said that he was able to throw his right leg over his shoulder like a bale of wood. Huddleston spent 36 years displaying his exceptionality for profit.

Robert Huddleston, eventually came to retire in Fremont where he continued his active lifestyle, restoring automobiles and raising rabbits. He passed away in 1970 after living his life to its fullest.

••

MIGNON

– The Penguin Lady

Mignon was born in the early 1900's, likely around 1910, with a condition called phocomelia. Phocomelia typically results in the stunting of limbs and the fusion of digits. In Mignon's case, her fingers were fused in such a way as to resemble flippers. Furthermore, as her truncated limbs forced Mignon to waddle rather than walk – her stage name, 'The Penguin Lady' was both apt and easily assigned.

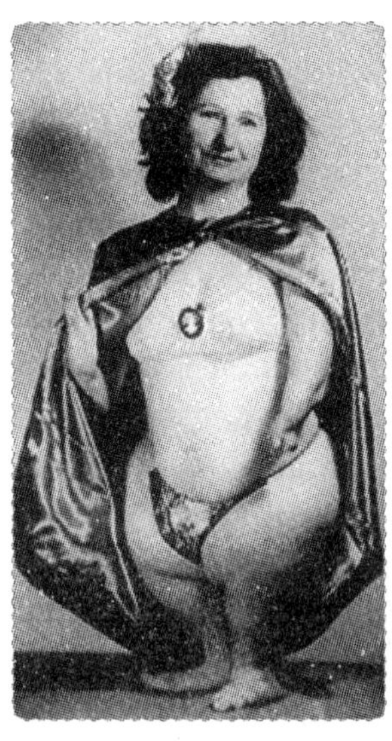

Her name, Mignon was not her birth name. Most reports indicate that her given name was Ruth. Mignon is the French word for 'cute' and she likely adopted it early in her career. In fact, for quite some time she was known as Mickey Mignon and even today her true surname is debatable.

While Mignon often wore a two piece bathing suit to show off her unique physique, she was not content to rely on appearance alone. She learned to play the rather exotic marimba, an African instrument similar to a xylophone. She proved to be very proficient as she was not only featured in numerous sideshows, her act was also featured at the 1933 Century of Progress Exposition in Chicago and the 1939 and 1940 World's Fairs in New York.

Mignon married twice in her lifetime. She had a healthy son with her first husband, a normal man by the last name of LaArgo and in the 1950's she married fellow sideshow performer Earl Davis, a gnarled and crippled former acrobat known as 'Hopp, the Frog Boy'. The two performed together for close to a decade.

Following her retirement in the 1960, Mignon disappeared from public view and the final chapters of her story remain shrouded.

ELLA HARPER

– The Camel Girl

Most sources indicate that Ella Harper was born in Hendersonville, Tennessee in 1873, though there are some conflicting reports. What is not argued, however, is the fact that Ella was born with an unusual orthopaedic condition resulting in knees that bent backwards. The nature of this unusual affliction is exceedingly rare and relatively unknown, however most modern medical types would classify her condition as a very advanced form of congenital genu recurvatum – also known as 'back knee deformity'. Her unusually bent knees, coupled with her preference of walking on all fours resulted in her moniker of 'The Camel Girl'.

In 1886, Ella was the star of W. H. Harris's Nickel Plate Circus, often accompanied by a camel when presented to audiences and she was a feature in the newspapers of every town the circus visited. Those newspapers touted Ella as the most wonderful freak of nature since the creation of the world and that her counterpart never did exist.

The back of Ella's 1886 pitch card is far more modest in its information:

"I am called the camel girl because my knees turn backward. I can walk best on my hands and feet as you see me in the picture. I have travelled considerably in the show business for the past four years and now, this is 1886 and I intend to quit the show business and go to school and fit myself for another occupation."

It appears that Ella did indeed move on to other ventures and her $200 a week salary likely opened many doors for her. After 1886, no further references to Ella, the Camel Girl can be found.

GRACE MCDANIELS

– The Mule-Faced Woman

Grace McDaniels was born in 1888, the same year when Jack – the Ripper was terrorising London, on a farm near Numa, Iowa to perfectly average parents. After winning an 'ugliest woman' contest in 1935, Grace joined up with F.W. Miller's sideshow.

Grace likely suffered from Sturge-Weber Syndrome. Sturge-Weber Syndrome is a genetic condition which, in Grace's case, caused a large port, wine coloured birthmark to thicken and distort the flesh of her face. Her condition was degenerative in nature and became worse with age. Shortly before her death, the fold of skin on her face hung more than four inches below her chin. Eventually, Grace had difficulty speaking due to the growth that enveloped her face.

Grace was very sensitive about her appearance. She often tried to hide her disfigurement with makeup and then later, as her condition worsened she took to wearing a veil. Grace also greatly disliked being called a freak and hated the 'World's Ugliest Woman' epithet used to advertise her appearances. She was often seen backstage covering her ears as not to hear the ballyhoo – the outside sales pitch and the talker calling her a freak and detailing her deformities. However, as time went on, she began to make a good living with the sideshow; she became more and more comfortable with her condition and position in life. Eventually, she was able to convince the talkers and promoters to refer to her by the moniker she was known – Grace McDaniels, the Mule Faced Woman.

Those who knew Grace said she was a wonderful and shy person. Later in life, Grace became a mother. A great deal was made of the event and for quite some time an almost fairytale mythology sprung up around the birth of her son Elmer. Contrary to those charming stories of love and marriage, the truth was that a carnival handyman allegedly named Johnny impregnated Grace while he was intoxicated and was never heard from again.

While Elmer was born a normal child, he grew into a physically and emotionally abusive alcohol and morphine addict who regularly stole from both Grace and from the sideshow to pay off dangerous gambling debts. Acting as his mother's manager, it wasn't long before sideshows stopped hiring Grace due to the reputation of her son.

The sad life of Grace McDaniels ended peacefully in 1958 and the true monster, her son Elmer, soon followed due to sclerosis of the liver.

BILL DURKS

– The Man with Three Eyes

Bill Durks understandably had a tough childhood. He was born in Jasper, Alabama on April 13, 1913 with a condition known today as frontonasal dysplasia. During gestation, the two halves of Bill's face failed to come together completely and uniformly and as a result he was born with deep cleft lip, open palate and a split nose. According to some accounts, Bill was also born with both of his eyes sealed with hoods of skin and his eyes were opened surgically when he was a small child.

Due to his appearance, Bill was denied an education. The school children would not accept him and his family was simply too poor to afford private schooling. Furthermore, by all accounts, the Durks family was ashamed of their son and didn't want him attending school anyway. As a result, Bill was a socially awkward and introvert man. To make things even more difficult for poor Bill, his cleft lip made him difficult to understand.

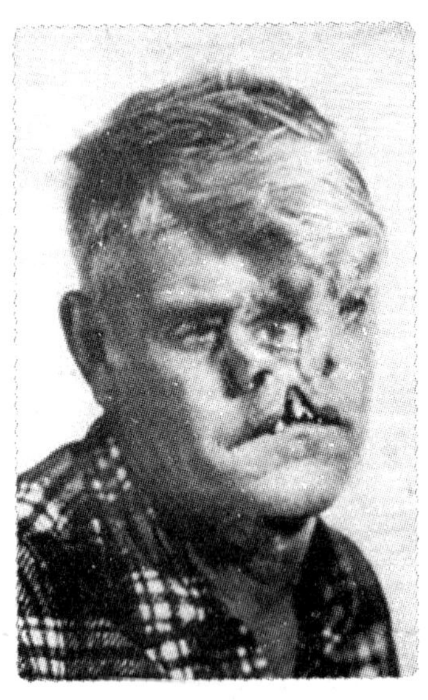

One day, in his early teens, Bill attended a local fair as a spectator. The showmen running the sideshow instantly invited him to go on tour and Bill left behind his bleak life for a chance at fortune and soon became the 'Man with Three Eyes'.

In an added bit of showmanship, during exhibits Bill would paint a third eye into the divot between his noses. Likely the fakery was not noticed during his career because few could stare Bill directly in his face. In a bit of irony, Bill, the man billed as having three eyes, was in reality the man with one eye as he was blind in his right eye.

Bill was quite a successful marvel and worked with numerous show including Kelly-Sutton Shows, Gooding's Million Dollar Midway, Hall & Christ Shows, James E. Strates Shows and Hubert's Museum making a good living. He was often taken advantage of and exploited due to his meek nature. Bill was also illiterate, which meant he could not read the contracts he signed.

Over time, Bill eventually became quite well liked by his fellow marvels. Many of them began to look out for his interests. Most notable wass the close friendship Bill developed with Melvin Burkhart, 'The Anatomical Wonder'. Burkhart took Bill under his wing and taught him how to interact with crowds, how to interact with people, gave him confidence and even taught Bill how to read. Bill began to love the sideshow and the crowds. He cherished the idea that while once he was shunned by society, now people were paying to see him. Bill quickly became the star of the show and spent the later part of his career with the Slim Kelly and Whitney Sutton shows. Bill was always grateful for the friendship he found in his fellow performers and his mentor Burkhart.

Burkhart eventually introduced Bill to Mildred the alligator-skinned woman. Mildred was born in 1901 and was a bit older than Bill but friendship quickly turned to love and, despite appearances, the two married. They spent several happy years together as the 'World's Strangest Married Couple' until Mildred passed in June 1968. Bill was completely heartbroken and soon retired to Gibsonton, Florida where he joined his beloved wife on May 7, 1975.

Bill Durks was a man who began his life hidden from the world by parents who were ashamed of him. He turned to the sideshow and found the love and friendship he lacked his entire life. It was love and friendship he deserved as a human marvel and a testament to the perseverance of man.

••

MAURICE TILLET

– The French Angel

Perhaps most well-known under the name 'The French Angel', Maurice Tillet was born in France in 1903 as a completely average and healthy child. He aspired to become an actor and was highly intelligent, allegedly speaking 14 languages and being quite gifted in prose. However, in his twenties, Maurice developed acromegaly.

Acromegaly is rather a rare hormonal disorder that occurs when the pituitary gland produces excess growth hormone. Usually, the condition is caused by a pituitary tumor, and results in bones growing wildly and uncontrollably. The word 'acromegaly' is derived from Greek and literally translates as 'large extremities'. Because the disease slowly progresses, it is difficult to diagnose in the early stages and is often missed for many years. In the case of Maurice Tillet, a diagnosis was long in coming and his body and face in particular were disfigured significantly. Unable to endure the constant gawking and humiliation, Maurice fled France.

In America, Maurice crafted a new identity befitting his disfigured appearance as a rough and villainous professional wrestler. Renamed 'The French Angel' and often called the freak ogre of the ring, Maurice was a great success finishing off adversaries with his patented Bear Hug. On August 1, 1944, 'The French Angel' defeated Steve 'Crusher' Casey for the American Wrestling Association World Championship.

Ten years later, on April 4th, 1954 Maurice died at the age of 51. In life, Maurice was a private and reclusive man, however, on his death bed, he gave permission to have a cast made of his face. One subsequent 'death mask' currently resides at the USA Weightlifting Hall of Fame inside the York Barbell Building in York, Pennsylvania.

••

MARY ANN BEVANS

– The Homeliest Woman

Mary Ann Bevans, commonly referred to as 'The Homeliest Woman in the World', likely suffered from acromegaly. She was born Mary Ann Webster in London, England in 1874 as one of the eight children. She was employed as a nurse and began to display characteristics of acromegaly shortly after her marriage in 1903.

Following the passing of her husband in 1914, she found herself solely financially responsible for her four children. In an attempt to make some money, she entered and subsequently won an 'Ugly Woman' contest.

She was quickly hired by Coney Island's Dreamland Circus in 1920 and there she remained, excluding a few short appearances for Ringling Bros. and a 1926 World's Fair, until her death at the age of 59 on December 26, 1933.

More recently, a Hallmark birthday card featuring the image of Mary Ann Bevans launched a feeling of outrage in UK shops. A Dutch doctor complained that the card was inappropriate. Hallmark realised their error and promptly removed the offensive cards.

PAULINE MUSTERS

– The Little Princess

In the history of the world, little Pauline Musters is the smallest mature woman ever officially recorded. Pauline is currently listed in the Guinness Book of World Records as having stood only 1 foot 11.2 inches in height.

Born on February 26, 1876 in Ossendrecht in the Netherlands Pauline Musters was almost half of her final height straight from her mother's womb. At birth, she was just over 12 inches. At age nine, the tiny dynamo weighed only three pounds and in adulthood Pauline Musters weighed less than nine pounds. She had curvy little figure and in truth she had no shortage of male suitors.

Pauline began her professional career as an infant at which time the public simply marvelled at her tiny proportions, but as she grew older Pauline took to performing as well. She was eventually known for being an adept acrobat and for skilfully dancing with partners drawn from the audience. As her performances progressed in quality, Pauline took on many unique stage names. She was perhaps best known simply as Princess Pauline and on par with her name she took to wearing remarkable elegant gowns on stage, with details and stitching so minute that the garments themselves were a wonder to behold.

During her career, Princess Pauline toured Belgium, Germany, France and Britain before being invited to perform in the United States in 1894. She debuted in New York City's Proctor's Theatre on New Year's Eve and stunned and thoroughly charmed the audience. She performed with a grace that moved those who saw her. She was a fairy, a tiny regal princess on a huge stage dancing out what she felt in her heart and it was beautiful. Princess Pauline quickly became the darling of New York.

Tragically, while Pauline's star burnt brilliantly, it expired far too quickly. Shortly after arriving in New York, the diminutive Princess contracted pneumonia and meningitis. Pauline Musters succumbed to illness on March 1, 1895 in New York and the world lost its smallest but greatest miracle.

••

CAROLINE CRACHAMI

– The Sicilian Fairy

Recently a number of television shows, documentaries and circulating picture sets have generated great interest in the genetic phenomena of primordial dwarfism. These tiny people, these seemingly fragile, delicate and near ethereal human beings conjure images of gossamer fairies and quaint folk stories. Such enchanting imagery is likely the root of this new interest in the condition.

The first individual to be medically cited with what we now call primordial dwarfism was Caroline Crachami. The story of 'The Sicilian Fairy' is inspiring, tragic and empowering all at once depending on which version of her biography one believes. Regardless, her story is one that should be told and remembered for it demonstrates the greed often found average men and chronicles the careless exploitation of a remarkable human being.

According to the pamphlet entitled *Memoirs of Miss Crachami*, the celebrated Sicilian dwarf Caroline Crachami was born at Palermo in Sicily on November 15, 1815. Caroline Crachami purportedly only weighed one pound at birth and measured a scant eight inches in height. Caroline was the only unique child of five siblings and despite claims of exhibitions in Panama, Miss Crachami first came to major public prominence during a visit to England in 1824. While there Miss Crachami was accompanied by one Dr. Gilligan who acted

as her agent and he exhibited her in Liverpool, Birmingham and Oxford before finally taking her to London where she was exhibited in Mayfair.

Crachami caused a great amount of sensation and proved to be incredibly popular. Hundreds of people would queue up daily and pay one shilling to view the nine-year-old, nineteen inch marvel. For the most part, inside the exhibit, Miss Crachami would simply wander around the stage while listening to music. For a few shillings more, one was permitted to handle the tiny girl, permitted to dance a little with her, to pat her head and feed her a biscuit or two. King George IV was an admirer as were three hundred members of the English nobility. More than three thousand members of high society visited and played with the doll-like Crachami and likely thousands more common folk did so as well.

The exhibiting schedule was gruelling and on June 3rd of 1824, after receiving more than two hundred patrons, the tiny Miss Crachami collapsed and expired during exhibition.

Her exhibitor, Dr. Gilligan, took Crachami's earthly remains to various medical institutions before selling them to the anatomist John Hunter for $500, and this was where the tale takes a tragic twist. Caroline was a child far younger than the nine years she was billed as. Modern examinations of her remains place her age at no more than three. She was also likely not Sicilian and probably hailed from Ireland where her parents read of her death in the Cork Inquirer. Her father quickly ferried to England in an attempt to halt any dissection and autopsy. However, he arrived too late and Caroline's bones had already been stripped bare.

The skeleton of Caroline Crachami now resides at the Hunterian Museum at the Royal College of Surgeons together with a few mementoes of her life including a pair of her silk stockings, her slippers, a ruby ring and casts of her face and arm. There Caroline forever stands next to The Irish Giant – Charles Byrne, his seven foot seven skeleton standing as a silent protector.

25 NICHOLI

– The Little Prince

Many have claimed to be 'The World's Smallest Man' but The Little Russian Prince may have actually lived up to that billing. Allegedly, the tiny man weighed less than sixteen pounds and stood only eighteen inches in height.

According to *A Sketch of the Life of the Russian Prince* – a lengthy biography found on the back of his pitch card, Nicholi was born in Siberia in the 1870's to a Russian Military Officer implicated in an assassination plot against the Czar. Found guilty, his father and mother were moved into a Siberian penal settlement and 14 months later, little Nicholi was born. He was discovered at the age of 28 when the Governor of the colony observed that the boy had never reported for mandatory military enlistment at the age of 21. When the tiny Nicholi was brought before him, the Governor was amazed. Eventually, the Czar heard of the tiny man and demanded that Nicholi be brought to him. While before the Czar little Nicholi begged so convincingly for the freedom of his family that stunned Czar granted his request.

Despite his well-padded biography, very little is known about Nicholi. His appearance is somewhat unusual when compared to other midgets of the era and there has been much speculation that Nicholi was not a midget at all. Rather, some believe that Nicholi was actually a child afflicted with the rare aging condition known as progeria.

Progeria causes children to undergo physical changes associated with aging but at a highly accelerated rate. Children afflicted loose their hair, teeth, and develop physical ailments and conditions commonly attributed to the elderly. Stunted growth and a fragile appearance are also major symptoms of the syndrome.

While Nicholi was billed as being in this mid-thirties, if he did indeed had progeria, he was likely no older than 10. Most people with progeria die before the age of 13. Thus, as his pitch card claims that Nicholi spoke Russian, Hebrew, English, and German – skills very unlikely in a 10 year old – his entire biography comes into question. The modern diagnosis does answer several questions and observations and would also explain Nicholi's sudden disappearance – he likely had a career of only one or two years.

It is also possible, and much more plausible, that Nicholi had primordial dwarfism. Most primordial dwarfs, in addition to being short in stature, also exhibit several skeletal and endocrine disorders. But the appearance is not unlike Nicholi's. Furthermore, on average, the lifespan of a primordial dwarf is quite short as well.

Finally, and perhaps most interestingly, there have been less than 100 confirmed cases of progeria since its discovery in 1886 while primordial dwarfism is more common, it is still quite rare. The Little Russian Prince, born in the 1870's, predated the discovery of one of the syndromes that possibly afflicted him. He may very well be the first photographed case of progeria.

••

JOSEF BORUWLASKI

– Midget Majesty

In his autobiography *Memoirs*, Count Josef Boruwlaski writes: "I was born in the environs of Chaliez, the capital of Pukucia in Polish Russia in November 1739. My parents were of middle size; they had six children, five sons and one daughter. Three of these children were above the middle stature, whilst the two others, like myself, reached only that of children in general at the age of four or five."

Toward the end of the seventeenth century it became incredibly fashionable for aristocrats and royalty to own a dwarf or midget for the purpose of entertainment. It was such a fad that Catherine de' Medici – the queen of France attempted to breed a pair of her court dwarves. Many more attempts were made, most notable of which was done by Peter the Great in 1701 when he staged a grand wedding between two dwarves – an event not only attended by his courtiers, but by foreign ambassadors as well. Therefore, one would expect the lives of those little people to be abject misery. However, the memoirs and life story of Count Josef Boruwlaski contradicts that assumption.

Boruwlaski was born a midget and into a very poor family. The financial situation only worsened when Josef lost his father at the age of nine. However, through good fortune his mother happened to be of limited noble blood and had a patron in wealthy noblewoman, the Staorina de Caorliz. She took a shine to the tiny lad and convinced mother Boruwlaski to send the young man to live with her and be educated. Her mother agreed and young Josef thrived in his new home. As a result, although he only stood two feet tall in his early teens, he possessed etiquette that would have shamed most artristrocrats and was a brilliant composer of music.

When the Staorina got married, Josef became the protégé of another even wealthier noblewoman, the Comtesse de Humiecka, and it is from there that Josef's life became even more interesting.

The Comtesse had a great lust for travel and brought Josef along. He was able to grace the courts of the highest crust of noble society. Maria Theresa – Her Imperial Majesty, Empress of Austria and Hungary – was so delighted to meet him that she gave him one of her own diamond rings. Prince Kaunitz, of Munich, gave Josef a pension for life. He also met and entertained the exiled king of Poland, King Stanislaus, and the Duc d'Orleans in Paris. When Stanislaus II acceded to the throne of Poland, he took Boruwlaski under his protection.

Josef eventually left the wing of the Comtesse and married a noble woman after being granted another pension and title by the Polish King. He fathered a daughter, wrote his autobiography, and settled in England where he toured and performed compositions for the public. He retired to Durham, England where he passed away on September 5, 1837 at the age of 98.

Perhaps his most interesting meeting occurred in a visit to London: "Soon after my arrival in London, there appeared a stupendous giant; he was eight feet four inches high, well proportioned and had a pleasing countenance, and what is not common in men of his size, his strength was adequate to his bulk; many persons wished to see us in company, particularly the Duke and Duchess of Devonshire. I went and I believe we were equally astonished. The giant remained sometime mute. Then stooping very low he offered me his hand, which I am sure would have enclosed a dozen like mine. He paid me genteel compliment and drew me near to him, that the difference in our size might strike the spectators the better; the top of my head not reaching his knee."

The giant is unknown although a writing of the times states that the man was named O'Brien and called himself the 'Irish Giant'. Believe it or not, there were at least four 'Irish Giants' parading about the United Kingdom at that time. Two of them were named O'Brien.

GRADY STILES JR.

– The Murderous Lobster Man

Grady Stiles Jr. is a rarity in the world of human wonders. By many accounts, this teratological terror was every bit the monster he appeared to be.

The Stiles family has been afflicted for over a century with ectrodactyly, a condition commonly known as 'Lobster Claw Syndrome'. It is a rare congenital deformity of the hand where the middle digit is missing and the hand is cleft where the metacarpal of the finger should be. This split often gives the hands the appearance of lobster claws although cases range in severity. Often this condition occurs in both the hands and tshe feet and, while it is an inherited condition, it can skip a generation. While the term ectrodactyly sounds medically sterile when compared to 'Lobster Claw Syndrome'. William Stiles was apparently the first in the family to display the condition in 1805. He was followed by Jacob Stiles, Elisha Stiles and Grady Stiles Sr. Grady Sr. was a sideshow attraction and when Grady Franklin Stiles, Jr., 'The Lobster Boy', was born in Pittsburgh on July 18, 1937 his father added him to the show at a young age.

Grady's condition was severe and he was unable to walk. He learned to use his hands and arms for locomotion and as a result, developed incredible upper body strength. He married twice and had four children. Two of those children, a girl – Cathy, and a boy, Grady III, were born with variations of ectrodactyly. Although the siblings were from different mothers, they sometimes toured together as'The Lobster Family'.

Grady had a dark side. He was known to be a highly abusive drunk. He often used his frightening strength to beat his wives and his children. When his oldest daughter Donna fell in love and got engaged with a young man in 1978, Grady didn't approve with her choice. Perhaps the young man stuck up for Donna, perhaps he confronted Grady. The night before the pair was to be married, Grady picked up a shotgun and murdered the young groom in cold blood.

The trial was a media circus. In the court Grady openly confessed to his crime and showed little remorse. However, he did not serve any time for the murder. He used his condition to his advantage. It was stated that since the prison system was not equipped to deal with his 'disability', confining him to such an institution would constitute cruel and unusual punishment. Grady was let off on 15 years probation. Following these events, Grady felt invincible. When he resumed beating his family one of his favourite taunts was – "I killed before and got away with it, I can do it again". Amazingly, during this time Stiles remarried his first wife Maria. She left her new husband, a sideshow dwarf, to remarry Grady and almost instantly regretted the choice. Eventually, the family had had enough. On November 29, 1993 Grady was gunned down by a hired assassin. The hitman was then 19 year old sideshow performer Chris Wyant, a neighbour to the Stiles family. He was paid $1500 in cash by Maria and her stepson Harry, to put three bullets into the skull of Grady Stiles Jr.

Wyant was convicted of second-degree murder and sentenced to twenty-seven years. Harry was considered the mastermind behind the plot. He was convicted of first-degree murder and sentenced to life in prison. Maria was convicted of conspiracy to commit murder and was sentenced to twelve years in prison. In her defence, Maria stated, "My husband was going to kill my family. I believe that from the bottom of my heart. I'm sorry this happened, but my family is safe now."

The family has carried on. Grady III has a daughter, Sara, who does not have ectrodactyly. Cathy married and has a lobster-clawed daughter named Misty. The three of them still perform on occasion. Cathy has taken up acting and has appeared in the series Carnivale and in Tim Burton's film *Big Fish*.

DOLLY DIMPLES

– The Dainty Fat Lady

While Dolly Dimples was not the most famous Fat lady or even the most rotund, her story is almost unparalleled in the history of sideshow.

She was born as Celesta Herrmann in Cincinnati on July 18, 1901. As a baby, her weight was average and her appetite was considered normal. It wasn't until early childhood that Dolly began to pack on weight. Her early weight gain was contributed to the visitations of a family friend. This friend happened to be a butcher and he often played a game with young Dolly that involved dangling bits of butchered meat in front of her. Dolly loved the game. She was influenced so much by it that her first word was 'meat'. Her fascination with food had begun and as she grew older, her appetite grew. Dolly would often stretch her allowance by buying day old baked goods and broken cookies. By the sixth grade, she weighed 150 and she never finished high school due to the harassment and bullying she had to endure daily. When she dropped out of school she was just less than 300 pounds.

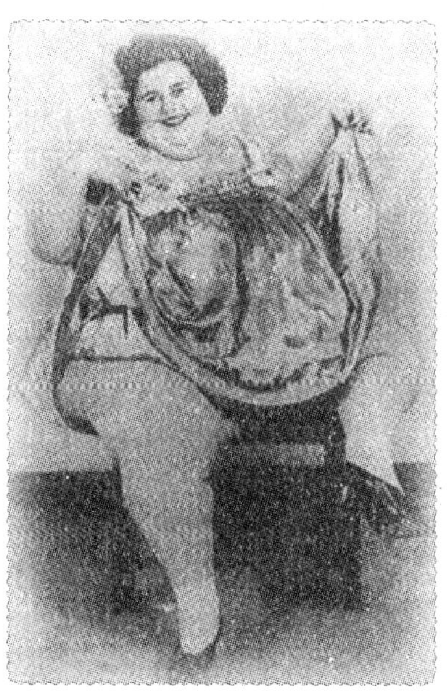

She met a man named Frank Geyer and, despite the fact that Frank was a slim and trim 135 pounds, he liked her and encouraged Celesta's appetite. She gained a further 100 pounds in one year and the pair eventually married.

In 1927, the couple went to visit the travelling Happyland Carnival just outside of Detroit. The carnival owner spotted the colossal Dolly and noted that she outweighed his advertised Fat Lady by at least 50 pounds. He offered her a job on the spot and she accepted almost immediately.

She took the name Dolly Dimples, sometime Jolly Dolly and she was billed as the 'World's Most Beautiful Fat Lady'. In an effort to become and even bigger attraction, Dolly began to ingest even larger quantities of food. Her daily diet also included pounds of potatoes, gallons of milk, multiple servings of meat and many loaves of bread. Her calorie intake was very close to 10,000, five times what is required daily. By the time she was touring with Ringling Bros. in the 30's, standing only 4 foot 11 inches, she weighted in at 555 pounds. The dresses she wore on stage consisted of twelve yards of fabric.

In 1950, Dolly suffered a near fatal heart attack. Her doctors told her to alter her diet or she would die. Dolly was frightened by the prospect of death, she enjoyed life greatly, and so she paid attention to the advice in a most astounding fashion.

In fourteen months, Dolly Dimples was gone, and in her place stood Celesta Geyer at a svelte 112 pounds. She had lost over 443 pound by limiting her diet to baby food. The Guinness Book of World Records recognises this achievement as the greatest weight loss in the shortest period of time.

The now 'Skinny Lady' spent the rest of her life as the first diet guru. She wrote a best selling book called *Diet or Die: The Dolly Dimples Weight Loss Plan* and followed by *The Greatest Diet in the World.*

She went on to run a small art gallery until her death in 1982.

••

GEORGE AUGER

– The Cardiff Giant

Captain William George Auger was Born in Cardiff, Wales on December 27, 1882 to parents of average size. By fourteen, George already stood over 6 feet in height. As an adult, Auger was often billed at standing over 8 feet in height, however his true stature was much more honest at around seven and a half.

As a young man, George Auger served as a police officer in Cardiff and was likely the tallest officer in the history of the company. Despite his enormous size, George was known for his soft demeanour, outgoing charm as well as his playful smile. He was known as an officer who would go the extra mile and was well liked by the public and his peers. From Cardiff, Auger moved to London where he found work as a 'Bobbie'. Due to his intimidating presence, he was often assigned to Queen Victoria's personal police escort squad. It was the Queen herself who began calling George as 'Captain' despite the fact that he was not a ranking officer. Her Majesty likely believed that a man with George's stature, personality and physical presence should be addressed with some formality and respect. The title stuck to Auger and he would be addressed as Captain for years to come – even by his work superiors.

When the Barnum and Bailey Circus toured London, Auger attended with his wife Bertha – all 5'4" inches – on his arm. When Auger stepped up to view the resident circus giant, he found that he stood a full head taller than the professional. This observation did not go unnoticed by the circus and Auger was immediately courted and offered employment. George did not hesitate as he was bored of police work and he loved the idea of seeing the world and entertaining the public.

Auger made it to America in 1903 and appeared as part of the Barnum and Bailey Circus at Madison Square Garden. To accentuate his size, management grouped Auger with the Hungarian Horvarth midget family. This practice was common in circuses and Auger did his best to ensure the family felt welcome. Auger and the youngest member of the family, Paul, quickly became best of friends. Auger eventually served as witness when Paul was married.

Not content to just be a circus giant, Auger decided to become an actor as well. In 1906, he wrote a play called *Jack, the Giant Killer*. The play premiered on the Orpheum vaudeville stage and Auger himself played the giant and the Horvarth midgets as the townsfolk. The show ran for nearly ten years due to its popularity. During that time, George also became an American citizen in 1911 and he did his best as a bond salesman in World War I.

By the 1920's, George considered himself retired. He and Bertha had a lovely place near Fairfield, Connecticut where he spent his days on the porch with his bulldog Ringling at his side. However, in 1922 George decided he had another tour left in him. He joined up with Ringling Bros., Barnum and Bailey Circus where he was paid $50 a week and loved every moment of it.

That same year, Auger was approached by silent film star Harold Lloyd in regards to playing a giant in the film 'Why Worry?'. As a film actor Augur would be paid $350 a week but more importantly, he would finally be a film star. Unfortunately, this final triumph was not to be.

On November 30th, while staying with friends in New Jersey, Auger complained of stomach pain shortly before drawing a pre-bedtime bath. His friends heard the gentle giant collapse in the bathroom but were unable to assist him as his body barricaded the door firmly closed. When the hinges were removed, the body of George Auger was discovered and mourned. ••

CHANG

– The Chinese Giant

Often billed as Chang Yu Sing, the gargantuan Chang Woo Gow was born in Fychow, China in 1845 and, before appearing in front of the Prince and Princess of Wales by request in 1864, the nearly eight-foot giant was best known for delighting the emperor of China as a part of his royal court.

It was unclear why Chang opted to leave the imperial court and visit England, but perhaps he knew there was a fortune to be had by exhibiting his 7 foot 9 inch frame. During his visit to England, the reception he received was beyond his expectations and quite literally thousands of curious patrons paid good money, up to three shillings each to witness the exotic giant speak and display traditional Chinese garb and etiquette. So great was the demand that what was initially planned as a brief visit eventually ballooned into a two year tour of England.

In the years following, Chang toured Europe with various promoters. Often he was exhibited on his own as a single attraction and sometime he was paired with a dwarf in order to accentuate his grand proportions. During his travels, Chang proved to be quite an intellectual marvel as he learned to speak several languages including English, German and French and developed an adoration of literature. During exhibition, rarely was a book far from his reach. Of course, rarely was anything far from his giant reach.

In 1881 the great P. T Barnum contracted Chang to his Greatest Show on Earth. At $600 a week Chang was one of the most well paid attractions of his time and he proved to be worth every penny. Aided by a Barnum advertisement campaign, the giant billed as being 'as strong as Heracles' and 'as beautiful as Apollo', Chang drew record crowds and hordes of admirers. In fact, despite being paired with a demure Chinese woman named King-Foo, hired to play the role of his bride, female admirers were persistent in their pursuit of the Chinese giant. The courting was so intense that Chang was forced to address his availability in nearly every interview he granted as it was always amongst the first questions reporters asked.

Chang was, of course, eventually smitten. While in Australia he met a young lady from Liverpool named Catherine Santley and he fell in love with her beauty, honesty and character. The couple married, had two sons and lived in China for a brief period before Chang moved everyone to Bournemouth, England.

Retired from exhibition, Chang purchased a Villa at 6 Southcote Road where he opened a tea house. There he displayed his many eastern curios and chatted with townsfolk including photographer William J. Day.

Admired and well liked for his character and kindness, Chang's peaceful life was magnificent until his beloved wife passed unexpectedly in 1893.

Four months later, at the age of only 52, Chang died of a broken heart. His funeral was a quiet affair as per his wishes. 50 of his closest friends gathered around his eight and a half foot plain oak casket to pay their respects. There, William J. Day summed it best when he described his friend Chang as 'a gentle giant, a giant of giants, great of stature, but with the kindest nature and a heart as true and tender as ever beat'.

••

ANNA SWAN

– The Giantess of Nova Scotia

Anna Swan was born in Tatamagouche, Nova Scotia on August 6, 1846. She was a large baby. She began her life at eighteen pounds and simply continued to grow. By the age of four, she was almost five feet tall. By the time she was sixteen, Anna towered over her parents and 12 siblings. When she was done growing, Anna stood a staggering seven feet, eleven and a half inches tall.

She began her exhibition career shortly after her seventeenth birthday. She started at the very top, working with P. T. Barnum in his New York Museum. Anna was often paired with the famous midget Tom Thumb to better accentuate both of their statures.

Anna made a great deal of money under the management of Barnum. Unfortunately, her career with the famous promoter was rife with disaster. The original Barnum Museum caught fire while Anna was on exhibit there and she barely escaped with her life. Trapped on an upper floor, Firemen were unable to carry her to safety. Instead, an outside wall was demolished and a crane was called to facilitate the rescue. When Barnum rebuilt his museum, Anna returned only to lose all of her possessions in a second museum fire. Anna quit the business for a time and returned to Nova Scotia. However, in 1869, Barnum invited her on a tour of the United States.

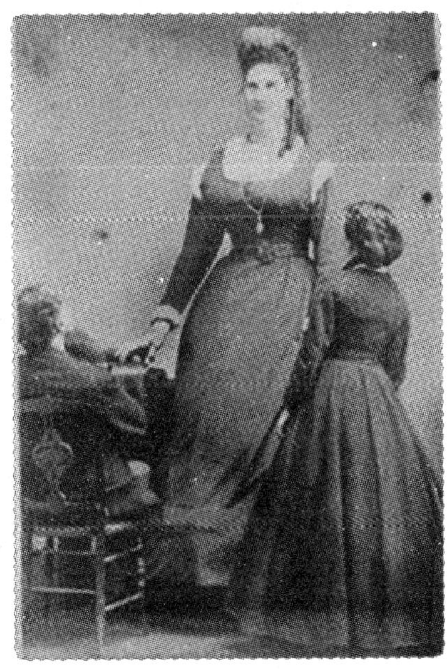

While on tour Anna met a Kentucky gentleman named Martin Van Buren Bates. Bates had been a Confederate Captain during the Civil War. He was charming, soft spoken and eloquent. He also happened to be nearly eight feet tall. The pair fell in love and married on June 17th, 1871. The pair, billed as the 'World's Tallest Couple' were showered with wedding gifts. Queen Victoria herself provided the gown and diamond ring.

The gigantic couple settled in Seville, Ohio and used their vast career earnings to build a colossal home. The ceilings were fourteen feet high, every door was at over eight feet in height and every piece of furniture was custom build for their frames. The pair continued to tour, but only sparingly.

In 1872, Anna gave birth to her first child. The little girl weighted eighteen pounds, just like her mother had, but unfortunately did not survive long after birth. In 1879, the couple had another child, this time a twenty-two pound boy. Sadly, he too did not survive past infancy.

Despite these tragedies, the two titans lived together in their custom home quite happily in love. In 1888, one day before her forty-second birthday, Anna passed away unexpectedly. Her husband, Martin, erected a great funeral monument to his wife. Atop her grave tower was a fifteen foot statue of a Greek Goddess.

Although Martin later remarried, he insisted that upon his death, he be laid to rest next to his beloved Anna and their children. His request was granted and today they rest together.

••

ROBERT WADLOW

– The Tallest Man

The tallest man in recorded history, Robert Wadlow, spent less than a year in the circus and none of it officially in the sideshow. Those who today watch over his legacy, are adamantly against associating Robert with the sideshow or the word 'freak'.

While Wadlow was a giant, he was far from being a freak. In fact, aside from his remarkable height he was beyond normal. He was a kind, intelligent man who is still remembered as a gentleman some 60 years after his passing.

He was the born of a normal sized couple and on February 22, 1918. By all accounts, Robert was a normal sized baby at eight pounds and six ounces but he quickly began to grow. Within twelve months he ballooned to just over forty-four pounds. At the age of five, he was five and a half feet tall and at the age of nine, he stood six feet and two inches.

His family was constantly hounded by showmen begging for a chance to display the human marvel. However, the Wadlow family insisted that Robert experience as average an upbringing as possible – given the circumstances. Wadlow even joined the Boy Scouts when he was thirteen and became the largest Boy Scout in history – he was seven feet and one inch and weighed 340 pounds.

In high school, Robert was popular and active in many extracurricular activities, even served as the advertising manager for the yearbook. He was completely accepted by his peers. However, when he attended college he lost that acceptance and struggled with the stares. It bothered him so much that he dropped out and returned to his parents quite penniless.

That was when his brief stint with Ringling Bros. began. His 1937 contract was brief and had strict conditions and terms. First, Robert would only attend shows at Madison Square Garden and the Boston Garden. He would display himself only two times a day for three minutes. He refused to allow any exaggeration of his height via media releases or standard height enhancing sideshow trickery like platform shoes, top hats and trick photography. Furthermore, Robert would only display himself in the centre ring and refused any association with the sideshow. Despite all of these restrictions, Robert proved to be incredibly popular.

Robert was so popular that following his time with Ringling Bros. he signed a fabulous contract with the International Shoe Company. The deal included quite a bit of travel and personal appearances and in just under a year Robert had made over 800 appearances and travelled over 300,000 miles. Perhaps most importantly, the company provided Robert with free shoes – a big deal when you are a size 37 and your shoes cost over $100 a piece.

Robert's feet always gave him a lot of trouble and due to the weight, they often formed blisters. Believe it or not, it was a blister that killed the gentle giant.

On July 4, 1940, Robert developed a blister. That blister became infected and Robert was unable to check into a hospital as they could not accommodate a man of his size. The infection progressed as Robert was attended to in a makeshift medical facility based in Robert's hotel room. Surgery, antibiotics and blood transfusions were not enough and Robert passed away on July 15, 1940 at 1:30am. He was only twenty-two and stood eight feet and eleven inches.

His funeral was attended by 40,000 mourners. It took twelve pallbearers to hoist his thousand pound casket. A life sized statue of Robert Wadlow still stands in his hometown of Alton, Illinois. It is a testament to a man who was the very definition of a human marvel.

33 HORNED HUMANS

– Wang, the Human Unicorn

Horned humans have a rich background in myth. Also, from the horns of Alexander to the horns of Moses, many important figures have been purported to possess horns. While in these cases the horns were a matter of misinterpretation or illusion, many notable naturalists and medical scholars have recorded occurrences of genuine horned humans. While technically not horns, human beings have been known to sprout horn-like outgrowths and many of these outgrowths have been located on the head. The earliest reliable account can be found in the report of German surgeon Fabricius Hildanus. In the late 1500's, he encountered a man with horns protruding from his forehead. Several other cases have been well documented by noted naturalists and medical experts. In his book, *Anatomicae Institutiones Corporis Humani,* Dutch naturalist Bartholinus mentions a patient with a horn measuring 12 inches and in 1696, there was a well-known case involving an old woman in France who had her amputated 12 inch horn presented to the King. There is also an account from around the same time regarding the extirpation of a horn nearly ten inches in length from the forehead of a woman of eighty-two. Finally, in 1886 the famous dermatologist Jean Baptiste Emile Vidal presented before the Academie de Medecine a twisted horn from the head of a woman. That horn was ten inches long. Several surgeons and naturalist recorded similar events and many went on to remove and actually collected the horns. There is one human horn 11 inches long and 2 1/2 in circumference currently in the collection of a London museum.

All told, before 1900, there were over one hundred confirmed cases of horned human beings. A correlation between ages and gender became apparent with elderly female cases being more common. Surprisingly, the horns would often begin growing back after being removed and there is one case in which the condition seemed genetic, with both a father and son displaying the condition.

Perhaps the most famous of all the horned marvels was Ripley's 'Human Unicorn'. In 1930, a Chinese farmer from Manchukuo was discovered by an expat Russian banker. The Russian was able to take a picture of the man and he sent the snapshot to Robert Ripley of 'Believe It Or Not!' fame. Known only as Wang, or sometimes referred to as Weng, the farmer was normal in every respect except fot the fact that he possessed a fourteen-inch spire-like horn growing from the back of his head.

Ripley offered a huge cash reward to anyone who could produce Wang for an appearance in his Odditorium. However, Wang disappeared from the public eye in the early 1930′s and was never heard from again.

The causes for human horns are varied. Most often it is attributed to benign calvarial tumours, such as osteomas, and an aggressive variant of a condition known as cornu cutaneum. It is important to note that 'horns' can grow anywhere on the human body but that the condition manifesting on the head only is a rarity. Today, horned human beings are practically non existent. There have been very few cases in the last one hundred years with modern medicine likely diagnosing and eliminating the situation before it grows into a real problem. Still, the occasional case does crop up.

••

ALICE DOHERTY

– The Minnesota Woolly Girl

The 'Minnesota Woolly Girl', Alice Elizabeth Doherty holds the unique distinction of being the only recorded American to be born with hypertrichosis lanuginosa. A condition exceedingly rare and unusual. Born with with a mane of fine and silky blonde hair, she was an American werewolf.

Alice was born on March 14,1887 in Minneapolis to average parents. The hirsute traits Alice exhibited were not typical of her bloodline. Her siblings were born sans mane and her parents were at a lost to explain why their baby girl was stricken with the condition. Her father Aloysius, in particular, found the situation difficult to comprehend but he soon noted that little blue-eyed Alice was a human marvel – one that the public would gladly pay good money to witness.

Alice Doherty began her career in exhibition at the age of two on a local level. Demand quickly dictated larger tours of the Midwest. By all accounts, Alice was a bright and playful child. She was as curious in spirit as she to behold. One admirer, a writer from Wisconsin, recorded that the toddler was "as frolicsome as a kitten" while another in Michigan declared her "the most miraculous baby ever born". By the age of five, the hair on her face measured more than five inches and by her early teens it was closer to 9 inches in length.

Alice was consistently a stand alone exhibit on display for extended periods of time in what was known as a storefront exhibition. It was a common practice for promoters or family members to rent commercial space in a busy city centre, set up an exhibit and sell tickets to the public before moving on to another city. Many predominant human curiosities earned their keep in this manner, most notably Joseph Merrick, and the Doherty family managed to earn a comfortable living from their unique daughter in this way as well.

Despite the fact that hypertrichosis was exceedingly rare, at the time Alice was touring in the late 1800′s, there was actually a substantial glut of contemporary hairy human wonders. Lionel – The Lion-Faced Boy (Stefan Bibrowski) and Jo-Jo – The Dog-Faced Boy (Fedor Jefticheiev) proved to be far more successful in both fame and fortune when compared to Alice Doherty. This was likely due to the fact that they had legendary promoters behind them as well as a certain exotic appeal. Alice, on the other hand, was a quiet American girl managed by well-meaning family members.

Alice was born with an unique visage, but inside she was the girl next door. Alice wasn't an entertainer, and her heart wasn't committed to becoming one. She was content to retire in financial comfort in Dallas in 1915 and it was there that she passed peacefully on June 13, 1933 at the age of 46.

35 BARBARA URSLERIN
– The Hairy Maid

Barbara Urslerin presents one of the earliest and most well documented historical cases of hypertrichosis on record. 'The Hairy Maid' was born in February of 1629 near the village of Kempten, Germany. She was purported to be the only member of her family afflicted with the mutation which was rather unique situation and quite different from the case of her nearest predecessor Petrus Gonzales.

All records indicate that Barbara was exhibited from a very early age. Her displays centred around her skill on the harpsichord, which she played happily and skilfully. Her existence was first confirmed in 1639 when anatomist Thomas Bartholin saw her exhibited in Copenhagen. Bartholin had opportunity to examine Barbara and he wrote that her entire body was covered with soft, blonde hair and a luxuriant beard.

In 1655, Barbara was documented in London and English writer John Evelyn visited Barbara there in 1657. He wrote that she was married to a German man by the name of Johann Van Beck and had one normal child. In 1660 records show that Barbara was touring France and her husband was acting as her agent. When she came to Beauvais, her husband applied to the local bailiff for permission to exhibit a 'strange prodigy of nature'.

In 1668, Barbara returned to London. She was examined there by the Dane, Holger Jacobsen. He hypothesised that Barbara was the result of a mating between woman and ape. His idea was outdated for even his time. His notes indicated that he examined her fully for any similarities to a monkey.

Following her 1668 visit to London, Barbara Urslerin disappeared from record. Given her unique appearance, this disappearance is incredible. Still, her final history remains unknown.

36 TAI DJIN

– Kung Fu Werewolf

Sometimes a story comes along that contains so many fanciful elements that one assumes it to be a work of fiction. Such is the story of Su Kong Tai Djin.

Tai Djin was born in China in 1849. He was born unique, afflicted with hypertrichosis. Unlike Jo-Jo, who was born a few decades later, Tai Djin was born into a highly superstitious family. As a result they saw his affliction as the work of demons and he was left in the forest to die.

A Shaolin monk travelling through the forest discovered the child and took him back to the Fukien Shaolin Temple. There Tai Djin was raised by the monks.

He was trained in martial arts and it quickly became apparent that he was exceptional in both appearance and ability. The boy must have been a sight practicing kung fu with his face covered in fine fur. He quickly became a favourite of many of the Shaolin masters and, as a result, each master passed their knowledge on to Tai Djin.

He was a sponge and mastered every technique shown to him. He became the first to master over 200 different empty hand systems and over 140 weapon systems. His various specialties included the infamous Chi Ma or Death Touch. After several years of extensive training, he became the first Grandmaster of Shaolin-

Do and one of the first to master all skills of the seven Shaolin temples. He became known as Su Kong Tai Djin. Su Kong simply means, Grandmaster.

Perhaps the most amazing part of the story is true. Su Kong Tai Djin was a real man, he really did have hypertrichosis and he was associated with Shaolin. Tai Djin was witnessed in the flesh by many, and revered by many more. He lived on for many years and passed away in 1928 after reaching a ripe old age and teaching others to be masters.

LIONEL

– The Lion-Faced Boy

Stefan Bibrowski was born in 1890 in Warsaw. He was discovered by a unknown German showman at the age of four and, with the permission of his parents, he began his exhibition career in 1895. He was given the name Lionel – The Lion-Faced Boy and a back story involving his mother witnessing his father being eaten by a lion was added to his biography. This was cited as the cause of his four inch long fur and the concept known as imprinting was a commonly held belief in the 1800's.

He did indeed have hypertrichosis and by all accounts was a very intelligent man who spoke at least five languages and had aspirations of being a dentist. Physically he was not an imposing figure as his official height was only five feet and three inches. Also, as is common with many forms of hypertrichosis, Lionel only had a couple of teeth in his mouth.

Lionel toured mostly in Europe but he did do several American tours – always with Barnum & Bailey Shows and once with Coney Island Dreamland Circus in New Jersey. He actually truly enjoyed the opportunities provided by his unusual hairiness. In fact, in 1904 in New York, the hotel he was staying at caught fire and Lionel was the very first man out. He was terrified of having his furry face singed. He was quoted as stating if that happened he 'would just be an ordinary man'.

Shortly after becoming a German citizen in 1932, Lionel passed away. He had no wife and children on record. According to some reports, he died in Italy and according to others, he died in a Nazi concentration camp – despite being a Catholic.

KRAO
– The Missing Link

Darwin's theory of evolution – and man's implied ascendancy from an ape-like creatures – is controversial. When it was first introduced to the public, most people thought the idea was preposterous. Until the apparent 'missing link' between man and ape appeared in a Philadelphia dime museum.

Krao was born in Siam, modern day Thailand, in 1876. From birth, the girl was completely covered with hair, including a mane-like track of hair flowing down her back from between her shoulder blades. She was discovered at the age of six by a promoter named the Great Farini. Farini took the girl on a successful tour of Europe before starting a tour in the United States. While the dime museum was a starting point, it wasn't long before Krao was a sought after marvel featured by the Ringling Bros. and Barnum and Bailey Circus.

While often called 'The Ape Woman', Krao was principally advertised as 'Darwin's Missing Link'. To all those who saw her, she was proof of Darwin's ideas. It was claimed, somewhat ridiculously, that Krao was of a race of tree dwelling, ape-like people but many bought the story including noted naturalists and scientists. Numerous papers were written on Krao and her role as Darwinian proof. In the 1896 tome *Anomalies and Curiosities of Medicine*, the authors noted her many ape qualities including her 'prehensile feet'. In reality Krao was a young woman of above average intelligence who was both well read and multilingual. She just happened to suffer from an advanced form of hypertrichosis.

Unlike Julia Pastrana, Krao was fortunate and she was never exploited. She performed and displayed herself in her own terms for most of her adult life. She was free to do as she pleased and spent the last 20 years of her life in a private apartment, entertaining guests and neighbours with her cooking and charming personality.

Krao never married, although she had admirers, and she passed due to influenza on April 16, 1926.

••

PETRUS GONZALES

– Wolf Boy of the Canary Islands

The sixteenth and seventeenth century must have been a simply enchanting time as fairy-tales seemed to spring into reality and the shelves of cabinets of curiosities overflowed with unusual items. The old stories of wee folk, giants and misshapen monsters seemed to be confirmed reality and in 1556, it seemed as though werewolves were also a factual entity when Petrus Gonzales stepped forward into the light of history.

Little is known of the parents of Petrus Gonzales as he was taken, as an infant, from his home in the Canary Islands to be presented to King Henri II in Pairs. Why was Petrus of such interest? Petrus Gonzales's entire body including his face was covered in long, wavy hair and he was an immediate medical sensation.

In 1557, the first formal report appeared, written by Julius Caesar Scaliger. In his report about the famed boy of Paris, Scaliger referred to the lad as Barbet – the same name used to identify a breed of shaggy dog. A second report in the same year confirms the arrival of Petrus in Paris and states that King Henri ordered that the furry boy should receive a formal education – not to be kind but rather out of curiosity – the King believed that Petrus was a savage and incapable of learning. His progress was monitored closely and he proved the King quite incorrect by not only learning the basics of education but also becoming fluent in the noble gestures, etiquette and tact. He became quite fluent in the language of the affluent, Latin, and took to wearing splendid robes that actually further accentuated his furry covered face. It was in this way that Petrus became a sought after court guest, a prodigy royal dignitaries and ambassadors flocked to see. He became a great asset to the court of King Henri and was rewarded for his service.

At the age of seventeen, in 1573, Petrus married a young French lady and by 1581 he was the father of two children. Both of his children, one son and one daughter shared his

unique appearance and the entire family became the most sought after curiosity of the era. In 1581, the family began a tour of Europe. In 1582 their portraits were painted in Munich by the order of Duke Albrecht IV of Bavaria. In 1583, the Gonzales family went to Basel where they were studied by the famed anatomist Felix Plater and he published a detailed account of the visit in his *Observationum* and further less detailed accounts followed the travels of the family until the early 1590's.

In the mid 1590's in Bologna, another detailed account updates much of the information on the family as the eight-year-old daughter of Petrus was the subject of an examination by Count Aldrovandi. The Count also commissioned a drawing of the family which now included Petrus, his twenty-year-old son and two young girls. It was assumed that his wife and eldest daughter had died.

The family seemed to break apart at this point and various members joined up with various European royal courts. A girl by the name of Tognina Gonzales, assumed to be the youngest daughter of Petrus came to public attention and the naturalist Ulisse Aldrovandi claimed in his *Monstrorum Historia* that Tognina was eventually married in the court of Parma and had several children of her own.

For the next 40 years, members of the Gonzales family ebbed and flowed from the course of history making brief appearance in noble courts. Considering their unique condition, it is unusual that more accounts and records do not exist. It is unknown what exactly happened to Petrus or his descendants. The last historical mention of a Gonzales can be found in a in a memorial plaque attributed to a Horatio Gonzales – an likely descendant of Petrus – and given to a certain Mercurio Ferrari.

KITTIE SMITH

– The Armless Dynamo

Katherine M. Smith, was born into a poor Chicago family on October 29, 1882. Like her two elder brothers and her younger sister, Kittie was rather an unremarkable girl and completely intact and average. That was until a sinister incident transpired and forever changed her life.

At the age of nine, Kittie's mother suddenly passed away and she was left in the care of her progressively abusive and alcoholic father. On the Thanksgiving Day the same year, Kittie tried to stand up for herself and refused to cook dinner for her father. Outraged, Mr. Smith beat Kittie and held her arms and hands against the stove. Despite her screams, Mr. Smith held his daughter to the red-hot stove until her arms were destroyed. Too badly damaged in the incident, both arms were eventually amputated three inches from the shoulder at Cook County Hospital. Kittie remained in serious care there until February of 1892.

The Humane Society prosecuted Mr. Smith to the full extent of the law but the jury failed to convict him due to lack of evidence. Kittie became a ward of the Children's Home Society of Illinois for several years, specifically living in the Home for Destitute and Crippled Children. It was in that home that one Dr. F. M. Gregg took an interest in the story surrounding Kittie and, as her father had by this time waived all rights and financial responsibilities, the good doctor created an education fund for Kittie. The 'Kittie Smith Fund' proved to be a success and the donations allowed the doctor to bring in specialised staff, perhaps even a sideshow performer to teach Kittie how to use her feet to accomplish common tasks. Kittie became adept in writing with her feet and loved to draw and paint. In addition, she could play the piano, type, and embroider silk. The fund also supported Kittie when she left in 1896 and paid for her board when she moved to Poynette, Wisconsin to attend public school.

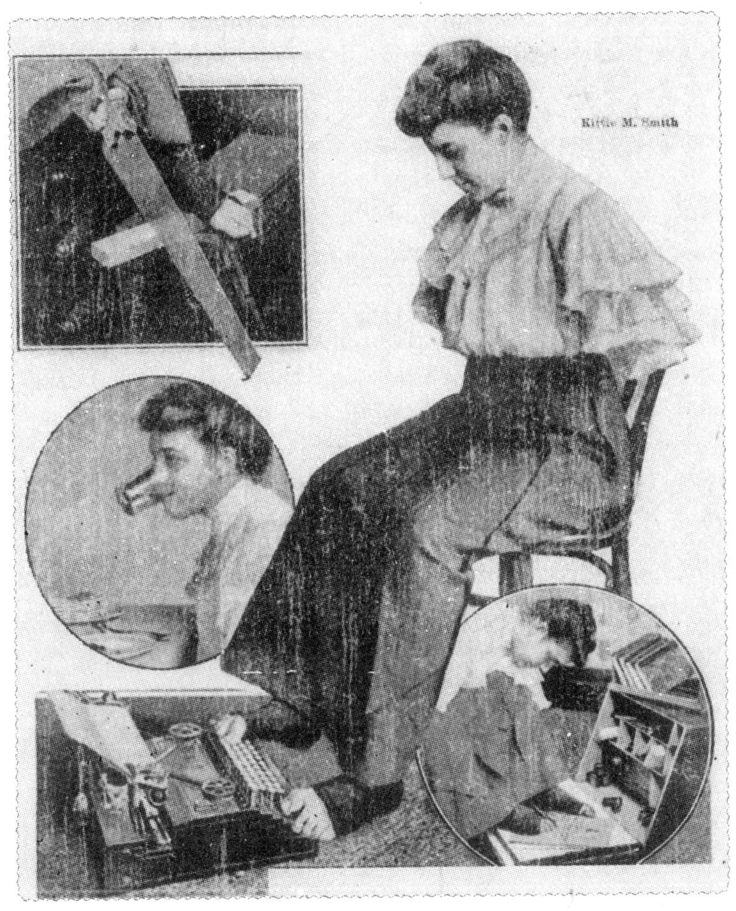

During this entire time, Kittie remained thankful and optimistic. She saw other children in the home far worse off than she was and was grateful for what she had.

By 1905, Kittie's fund was exhausted and at the age of 21 she was no longer eligible to draw from the state. Her father had passed away, her brothers were low paid labourers and her sister had been adopted. Kittie resolved to support herself and began to humbly capitalise on her tragedy by selling drawings and autobiographical pamphlets. The pamphlets she distributed were accompanied by a return card with a slot for a quarter. Upon receiving the pamphlet, the recipient would read her story and pay only if they were moved to do so. Something about the optimism and determination of the young girl resonated with the public and by March of 1906, Kittie had amassed over $35,000 in quarters.

That outpouring of support remains a testament to human sympathy and charity. An event compounded by the fact that Kittie had long ago forgiven her father and falsely claimed in her pamphlets that she lost her arms due to her own folly, by falling into a fire.

Kittie founded the Kittie Smith Company where she employed a bookkeeper, stenographer and dozen envelope stuffers. She aspired to help children with disabilities overcome their handicaps and displayed a remarkable set of skills to illustrate that nothing was impossible. In 1913, under Illinois' new women's suffrage law, Kitty was the first woman in Chicago to cast a ballot and she did so using only her feet.

In the 1930s, Kitty was still inspiring people by exhibiting her wide array of remarkable skills at Coney Island and with the Ringling Bros., Barnum & Bailey. Shortly thereafter, she quietly slipped into the background and retired.

••

CHARLES TRIPP

– The Armless Wonder

During his time, Charles Tripp was not only the most well-known armless wonder, he was also one of the most famous Canadian entertainers of his era. Born in Woodstock, Ontario on July 6, 1855, Charles Tripp owed much of his fame to his performance partner and dear friend Eli Bowen.

Charles Tripp was born without arms. But, as a young boy, he quickly adapted and became phenomenally adept at using his legs and feet as competently as a fully formed man would use their arms and hands. He was never exhibited during his youth but was well-known locally for performing mundane daily tasks in extraordinary ways.

As a young man, Charles Tripp grew restless in his small hometown. As fortune would have it, at the age of seventeen, Charles heard of a showman in New York who exhibited special people with unusual talents. Seeing this as his opportunity for fame and fortune, Charles Tripp packed his bags and headed to New York determined to meet the showman. All he had was a name, but that proved to be more than enough. The showman was P.T. Barnum.

Upon his arrival in New York, Tripp located Barnum's office and marched in unannounced. Barefoot, he demonstrated his morning routine by combing his hair, folding his clothes and putting his socks on. Barnum hired Tripp immediately. His career lasted more than fifty years.

Tripp performed many feats during his various exhibitions. Initially, most were of the daily mundane variety. His daily shave was always a crowd pleaser. But as Tripp grew into a learned and well travelled man, his repertoire reflected his maturity. Eventually, Tripp became well-known for his elegant penmanship, woodcarving, paper crafts, painting and photography.

Charles Tripp spent the bulk of his career touring with Barnum and eventually Ringling Bros. and Barnum & Bailey shows. Tripp was able to command as much as $200 a week during these tours, a figure supplemented by sales of his autographed cabinet cards.

It was during his partnership with Eli Bowen that Charles Tripp was truly able to attract public attention. Pairing an armless man with a legless one was surely a stroke of showman brilliance but it was a moment of jovial playfulness that would cement Tripp and Bowen into history. While the pair posed for promotional photographs, one of them spotted a tandem bicycle. In no time, the two not only mounted the bicycle built for two, but rode off together laughing as boys would. The photographer quickly snapped the pair mid-ride and the resulting surreal photograph still draws perplexed smiles.

Tripp married late in life, in his early seventies. Following the marriage, he limited his touring to North American states. Aided by his wife, Charles Tripp toured until the day he died. In January of 1930 Tripp passed away due to asthma in Salisbury, North Carolina. He was seventy-four years old.

ELI BOWEN

– The Legless Acrobat

The remarkable Eli Bowen was born in Ohio on October 14, 1844 as one of the ten children. While his siblings were physically average, Eli was born with his disproportional feet attached directly to his pelvis. In essence, Eli Bowen was a man born with feet but no legs.

Despite his physical configuration, or perhaps because of it, Eli strived to live an extraordinary life. He endeavoured to not only overcome the limitations of his deformity, but strived to be the best in a profession known for its perfect physiques and physically taxing routines. Eli Bowen wanted to be an acrobat.

Eli learned early to use his arms and hands to compensate for his lack of legs. Eli would hold thick, wooden blocks in his palms and use them as 'shoes', elevating his torso in order to walk on his hands. As a result of that process as well as steady farm labour, Bowen developed enormous strength and even in adulthood, he was able to navigate his 140 pound frame anywhere he chose. He started his professional career at the age of 13 in various wagon shows before eventually touring independently, performing in dime museums and finally touring Europe with Barnum and Bailey Circus. He garnered a reputation for being a magnificent and effortless tumbler and acrobat and for his phenomenal feats of strength.

Billed as 'The Legless Acrobat', Eli Bowen was known for his remarkable tumbling abilities but was applauded internationally for his extraordinary routine known simply as 'the pole routine'. While Eli stood only twenty-four inches in height, he had no reservations about climbing a thirteen foot pole in order to balance on a single hand at its peak. Gripping the pole, Eli would stretch his torso straight, parallel to the ground, and spin around the pole. Eli would then hold himself parallel to the pole using only his right arm. The routine not only displayed Bowen's strength, but was also unusually graceful. Soon, Eli Bowen was commanding a salary of over $100 a week.

As he grew into adulthood, Eli Bowen also became well-known for his handsome looks and at one point, he was considered by many to be the most handsome man in show business.

Eli Bowen's good looks drew many female fans to his performances. At the age of 26, Eli married 15-year-old Mattie and together he eventually fathered four healthy sons. He took great pride in his family and the majority of the photos featuring Eli feature his family as well. In fact, as Eli was so regularly photographed, a collector can actually watch his children grow into young men and eventually, adults.

Bowen continued to perform into his 80's simply because he loved performing. His sons were prosperous, one became a merchant and another became a lawyer and Eli owned property, specifically two farms in Michigan, and so money was never much of a concern. Eli simply loved life in the public eye and could not give up performing.

On May 2, 1924, Eli Bowen passed of pleurisy just days before a scheduled performance for The Dreamland Circus at Coney Island. During his long career, he was regarded with great reverence by his fellow performers. They lovingly referred to him as 'Captain Eli'.

DICK HILBURN

– The Quarter-Man

On January 15, 1918, an infant named Dick Hilburn was born in Bladenboro, North Carolina. He was born physically incomplete.

Dick Hilburn was born with a single arm and physically little else. He possessed no left arm and no legs, only a vestigial two-toed foot protruded from his left hip. Despite what would normally be considered a crippling handicap, Dick Hilburn possessed an unconquerable spirit and indomitable work ethic which allowed him not only to surpass expectations but also to exceed the ambitions of many able-bodied men.

Dick Hilburn conquered his mobility limitations with little more than a rolling board. He used his arm to propel and steer his body and in the process developed great physical strength. That strength allowed him to hoist his body wherever he wanted with relative ease.

Having dealt with his mobility issues, Hilburn focused on developing his mind and ingenuity. He proved to be a talented artist and became fairly well-known for his skills with a tattoo needle. He was also sought after as a commercial painter of signs, banners, trucks and semi trailers.

He possessed a natural business sense and rather than rely on showmen for exhibition purposes, Hilburn developed and operated his own show. He exhibited himself on his own terms and later, added a second attraction – a young parastremmatic dwarf, a dwarf with twisted limbs, named Carl 'Frogboy' Norwood. During the off season, the two operated a local diner, which was also owned by the one-armed wonder Dick Hilburn.

Successful in life, art and business, Hilburn was also successful in love. He later married an average woman who had all her fingers and toes.

Dick Hilburn ran his sideshow until the day he died in June of 1971. He lived his life as any man free of handicap would. His only limitation in life was his mortality.

As for Carl Norwood, he was managed by Hilburn's widow for a short time before joining up with the great showman Ward Hall. He toured for a few more seasons before retiring and passing on in Atlanta on February 24, 1976.

SARAH BIFFEN

– The Limbless Artisan

The remarkable case of Sarah Biffen began with her birth in October of 1784. She was born without arms and only vestigial limbs to a family of farmers in Somerset. Despite this perceived handicap, Biffen learned to not only perform simple tasks, but to perform extraordinary feats of dexterous artistry as well.

At the age of twelve, the Biffen family contracted their unwanted daughter to a showman named Mr. Dukes. Dukes exhibited Sarah throughout England and it was during these travels that he taught the young lady how to paint. It was initially done to improve her value as an attraction as the public loved to observe unique people accomplish rather mundane tasks. It was a precedent set long before by other limbless attractions. Crowds would gasp at the sight of limbless marvels brewing tea, shaving or firing pistols with accuracy. While Mr. Duke's greatest expectation was to have Sarah churn out a sketch or two, her artistic talent far surpassed any expectations.

The paintings of Sarah Biffen progressed steadily in skill, precision and beauty. Soon people flocked to watch her paint, perched upon a pedestal, and they paid large admissions for the privilege. During her early years, Biffen was best known for producing landscapes and miniature painted portraits on ivory cameos and medallions. She sold her creations for three guineas each and she could hardly keep up with the demand.

During her appearance at St. Bartholomew's Fair in 1808, the Earl of Morton paid Miss Biffen a visit. The Earl had heard of the 'Limbless Wonder' but was not prepared for the talent the girl possessed. In fact, the Earl was so impressed that he sponsored Sarah and made possible private lessons from Royal Academy painter, William Craig. From there, her popularity soared. Her paintings were eventually accepted into the Royal Academy and The Society of Artists awarded her a medal in 1821. The Royal Family commissioned her to paint their portraits in miniature and she did so for Queen Victoria among others. Also with the aid of her benefactor, the Earl, Sarah set up a studio on Bond Street in London.

Sarah Biffen became so famous that Charles Dickens mentioned her in Nicholas Nickleby and Martin Chuzzlewit. She fell on hard times in 1827 when her friend and benefactor, the Earl of Morton passed away. However, Queen Victoria soon awarded her a Civil List pension and she retired to a private life in Liverpool. She made a brief return some 12 years later, under the married name of Mrs. Wright, but her popularity never again reached its previous fervour.

Sarah Biffen died on October 2, 1850 at the age of 66. She was buried in St James Cemetery in Liverpool.

MADEMOISELLE GABRIELLE

– The Half-Woman

Mademoiselle Gabrielle was a legless marvel from the early 1900's. She was born in Basel, Switzerland in 1884 and began her exhibition career at the Paris Universal Exposition in 1900 as the Half-Woman.

Her first foray into show business proved quite successful as she soon travelled to America to work with the Dreamland Circus Side show, Ringling Bros. and Barnum & Bailey. Furthermore, in 1912, Mademoiselle Gabrielle embarked on a short-lived vaudevillian career with New York's Hammerstein Theatre. She eventually broke her contract with the theatre agent and was subsequently sued for breach. A four year court battle resulted in a $2000 fine paid to the theatre agent. Few human wonders appeared on the vaudeville stage, the Hilton sisters did so several years later, but Mademoiselle Gabrielle was a special case. She was beautiful, charming, graceful and demure enough for the general public to accept her deformity objectively.

Mademoiselle Gabrielle possessed no legs and, according to a 1929 London Life article, she possessed no stumps whatsoever. Her torso finished just below the hip gracefully. Her figure was impressive and she accentuated her physical qualities and natural beauty with opulent Victorian garb and striking jewellery. Mademoiselle Gabrielle was independent and never complained of her condition.

She firmly believed that she was ‘no less a woman’, despite being physically half of a woman.

Mademoiselle Gabrielle attracted men in droves and married at least three times during her lifetime. First, she was married to a man with the surname of Hunter and lastly to a German gentleman. Due to these surname changes, her later history is difficult to trace and her eventual date of demise is currently unknown.

STANLEY BERENT

– Sealo, the Seal Boy

Stanislaus Berent was born in Pittsburgh, Pennsylvania, on November 24, 1901. Stanley's stunted arms, a condition known as phocomelia, were due to a genetic fault and likely not due to chemical exposure. Phocomelia is a common defect associated with exposure to the drug thalidomide. Over 10,000 children were born with severe malformations due to prescription of the drug during the 50's and 60's.

According to many accounts, Stanley was discovered selling newspapers. He went on to appear in every major sideshow and dime museum in the United States. Calling himself 'Sealo', as phocomelia literally translates to 'seal arms', his performance consisted of completing mundane tasks without the use of full limbs. An ingenious stick and hock device often allowed Sealo to complete nearly any task. Furthermore, what truly set him apart from the other limbless marvels was his spectacular personality. He was loved by everyone, from colleagues to spectators and even members of the animal kingdom. While touring with Ward Hall, Sealo befriended a young chimpanzee. When spectators mocked or

teased Sealo, the chimpanzee was known to attack them. Perhaps due to orthopedic issues, or just a matter of comfort, Sealo often stayed in hotels rather than on the camp of the fairgrounds like many other performers. This practice, which may have seemed elitist, was simply accepted by his peers and no issue was ever made of it. Again, his character likely got him off the hook.

In 1972, Ward Hall's show came under attack from a political correctness group who believed the workers were being exploited. An obscure 1921 Florida law that banned the exhibition of the 'handicapped' was cited. Sealo, Ward Hall and a band of performers sued the State of Florida and the law was eventually repealed.

In 1976, Sealo retired to Gibsonton and eventually returned to Pittsburgh when his health began to falter. He passed away in 1980. His career spanned over 30 years.

CARL UNTHAN

– The Armless Fiddler

Carl Herman Unthan was born on April 5, 1848 in Sommerfield, East Prussia. Some stories claimed that he was nearly smothered by the delivering midwife, a popular narrative in the birth accounts of many marvels, and that he was rescued by his father before the evil deed was done.

It was his father who pushed young Carl to use his feet as one would use hands. Before long, the boy was able to grasp objects and write legibly. In his early 20's, Unthan began to learn the violin and quickly became very adept at playing the instrument with his feet. In addition to touring the globe, he was also invited to play before Strauss in Vienna.

Early in his career as a vaudevillian performer, his performance was similar to other limbless marvels. Often he would perform various mundane tasks like shuffling cards and smoking cigarettes and he made these tasks amazing by using only his feet. However, Unthan's ability with music soon took precedent and he was recognised more as a legitimate musician than odd exhibit.

During WWI, Carl was served with the German Army in a moral role. He would visit hospitals and demonstrate his abilities to recent amputees affirming that their lives were not over due to the loss of limbs. He even starred in a film which showcased his lack of physical limitations.

In 1928, at the age of 80, Carl Unthan passed away as a fulfilled and wealthy man. In 1935, his autobiography *The Armless Fiddler* was published and world remount for a second time.

NIKOLAI KOBELKOFF

– The Human Trunk

Born on July 22, 1851 in Siberia, Russia, Nikolai Wassiljewittsch Kobelkoff was the fourteenth child of normal parents. He was born without limbs, as a living torso.

Despite the murmured superstitions surrounding the young Nikolai, he was eventually befriended by a kind schoolmaster and he was able to obtain a proper education. Having no hands to grip a pencil, Nikolai adapted and was soon able to write by holding a pencil under his chin. His right stump proved useful due the fact that it was rather bony. Eventually, his technique proved to be quite accurate. He eventually even took up painting.

In 1871 Nikolai began his exhibition career in St. Petersburg. His initial venue lasted two years. Like many limbless marvels, his exhibition consisted of mundane tasks accomplished via extraordinary dexterity. His most notable feat was threading needles before awed audiences. In later exhibitions, Nikolai would simply paint. This was likely a rare instance where watching paint dry was entertaining. He also sometimes ate a full meal in front of the audience, even pouring the wine himself.

During his exhibitions, he would also display his means of locomotion, which was much more dynamic then many other limbless marvels. While he would sometimes crawl about like the later Prince Randian, he was incredible limber. He would often leap on and off chairs and even hop down flights of stairs. On occasions, Nikolai would also perform a headstand.

Nikolai was also a powerfully built man, despite the lack of limbs. On rare occasions, he would demonstrate his strength by perching an audience member on his stump and lifting them.

His great success in St. Petersburg warranted a tour. Eventually, Nikolai performed in every major European countries and for many notable nobles. While performing in Austria in 1875, he met a Viennese woman named Anna Wilfert and the two were married the same year in Budapest. The couple had their first child in June of 1876. Ten more followed and all were average in appearance.

Nikolai died in January 1933 as a wealthy and accomplished man. In 1898, Nikolai produced the short film *Kobelkoff* which documented his act. He published a memoir. His nude photo still elicit conversations. He was even able to buy his own amusement park which his descendants continued to run.

JOHNNY ECK

– The Half-Man

On August 27, 1911 Amelia and John Eckhardt welcomed the birth of twin sons. The two would have been nearly identical if little John Jr. had been born with legs. While Robert was completely formed, John Jr. was a perfectly healthy half-boy, seemingly 'snapped off at the waist'.

The brothers grew up in Baltimore and John proved to be incredibly self sufficient. By the age of one, he was walking around on his hands, before his brother was even standing. As Johnny grew older, his agility and independence amazed family and friends. In 1923, while attending a magic show at their local church, Johnny shocked the performing conjuror John McAslan by nimbly scampering onstage when a volunteer was requested. McAslan saw great profit in the half-boy and he managed to convince the Eckhardt family into signing both Robert and Johnny to a one year contract. McAslan later changed the terms of the contract by adding a zero to the duration.

Despite that bit of dishonesty, the brothers enjoyed their time in the magic game. The boys were later even a part of what was likely the most shocking illusion ever. Illusionist and hypnotist Raja Raboid developed a show in which he would recruit Robert from the audience for a hypnosis stunt. During the illusion, Robert would be placed in a box and be discreetly switched with Johnny and a dwarf wearing trousers hiked over his head. Raboid would then perform a variation of the old routine, 'sawing a man in half' and, when the box was opened, Johnny would commence chasing his 'legs' around the stage.

Stage hands would round them up and Raboid would reconstitute the body. Robert would then threaten to sue before storming off the stage. While the illusion was intended to be lighthearted and humorous, the site was often horrific to members of the audience. Fainting was common.

Johnny was a true entertainer who loved everything about show business. While in the circus he was often entertaining enough to be a single featured attraction. He was known for his impressive acrobatics, including his famous one-armed handstand, but he also juggled and trained animals. He was also an accomplished runner and was sometimes even called 'The Legless Runner'. Ripley called Johnny as 'The Most Remarkable Man in the World'. While Robert was incorporated into almost every appearance to better enhance the unusual physique of his brother Johnny, he was a talented performer as well. When not performing, the brothers conducted their own orchestra in Baltimore and were heavily involved in the arts. Johnny developed into a talented painter. In 1932 Johnny appeared in the movie *Freaks*. He impressed many with his performance and went on to appear in three Tarzan movies. However, following these films, Johnny decided to retire from show business. He and his brother opened a little amusement park featuring a tiny train, on which Johnny acted as conductor. Johnny was also able to make a comfortable living with his screen painting artwork.

Johnny was an outstanding human being who defined the term 'human marvel'. He was never ashamed of his appearance and overcame the handicapped label that was pinned on him at birth. Johnny loved his interactions with the average person and delighted in illustrating how one should not judge character based on appearance alone.

However in 1987, after being assaulted in his own home by a group of thieves, the aged Johnny became disgruntled with society and lost faith in man. Following the incident Johnny spent his remaining years in total seclusion stating that 'the real freaks were outside his home'. On January 5, 1991, after years in seclusion, Johnny suffered a fatal heart attack and died. His brother Robert followed him in 1995, aged 83.

FRIEDA PUSHNIK

– The Little Half-Girl

Frieda Pushnik was born without arms and legs on February 10, 1923 in Conemaugh, Pennsylvania. She claimed that her condition was due to a botched appendectomy conducted on her pregnant mother. The validity of this statement was questionable, however considering no lawsuit was filed – the story was most likely a case of sideshow creativity.

Frieda was a testament to human willpower. By all accounts, she never considered herself disabled. She accepted her condition as a matter of fact and strived to live as everyone else did. Her mother was the driving force behind this aspiration and it wasn't long before Frieda was feeding herself, sewing, crocheting and playing as children do. Remarkably, by holding a pen between her shoulder and chin, Frieda was not only able to write legibly but she actually won several awards for penmanship. Because Frieda was limited in movement, her mother would carry her to school daily and her brother or sister would carry her back.

In 1933, Robert L. Ripley of 'Ripley's Believe It or Not!' heard of Frieda and visited her and her family. He illustrated her story in one of his nationally syndicated cartoons, calling her 'The Little Half-Girl', and he eventually asked her to appear at the World's Fair in Chicago in 1933.

At the age of nine, accompanied by her mother and sister, Frieda began appearing in Ripley's 'Odditorium' with fellow child marvel Betty Lou Williams. Her act was little more than an introduction and a demonstration of her typing and writing skills but audiences were completely floored. She would repeat the five-minute show many times each hour through what was often a 16-hour day. In the six years she was on tour with Ripley, she was seen by millions. To make extra revenue, she would sell her pitch cards – a variety of portait photos. For a few dollars more she woould personally sign her photos.

After a brief retirement, she joined up with Ringling Brothers and Barnum & Bailey Circus. Her sister and mother again joined her. This time her sister actually performed with the circus as a skilled trapeze acrobat and dancing girl and even her mother worked for the circus office as a secretary. In 1944, the circus suffered a spectacular fire which claimed the lives of 167 people. Frieda was luckily carried to safety by a member of the minstrel show.

Despite that frightening experience, Frieda returned again to the circus and continued to perform until 1955, when 'politically correct' laws effectively forbid the display of human wonders and killed her livelihood. She retired to Costa Mesa California – fairly well off financially – where she lived quietly, adorning her home with her own oil paintings.

On Christmas Eve, 2000, the remarkable live of Frieda Pushnik ended. She passed away at the age of 77 – the victim of bladder cancer. She had never married, and despite being out of the public eye for decades, the news of her passing was the subject of many news stories. Even in death, 'The Little Half-Girl' remains a testament to human spirit.

PRINCE RANDIAN

–The Human Caterpillar

The man who became Prince Randian was born in 1871 in Demerara, British Guiana to Indian slave parents. Despite being born without arms or legs he was incredibly self-sufficient.

Randian was brought to the U.S. in 1889 and, while he performed at many dime shows and museums, he gained most of his fame performing for P. T. Barnum. In front of the large crowds, Barnum provided Randian demonstrated the ease in which he was able to shave, paint, write and even roll cigarettes. Not only was he able to roll a cigarette, he was also able to pull a match from its box, strike it, and light his freshly rolled cigarette.

Randian had many nicknames during his career. Randian's typical costume consisted of a striped woollen garment and his main mode of transportation was writhing about on the ground in a worm-like fashion. These two visuals led to his most common nickname, 'The Human Caterpillar' and he went on to appear in a variety of carnivals and sideshows, including Coney Island, for a forty-five year stint.

Randian had a role in the 1932 film *Freaks*, in which he demonstrates his cigarette rolling skills and utters a single unintelligible line. Oddly enough, it was said that he spoke several languages including Hindi, French, English and German.

By all accounts, he was a bright and charming man with a great sense of humour. Both of these talents helped him in getting a wife and make use of his one remaining appendage. He and his wife had five children.

Eventually Radian retired in Paterson, New Jersey and in 1934 he died at age 63 of a heart attack following a comeback performance.

Call him what you like: The Living Torso, The Snake Man, The Human Worm, The Human Cigarette Factory or The Amazing Caterpillar Man. Radian was a man who, despite his physical limitations, truly lived live to his fullest.

FRANCES O'CONNOR

– The Living Venus De Milo

The promise of suggestive sexual content lured many warm blooded men to curiosity displays, carnivals, and sideshows. The Cooche Shows (exotic or burlesque shows) presented by carnivals in the first half of the 20th century proved incredibly successful. But the shy or modest man would often opt to take in the sideshow, where skin was often available for viewing in a more discreet situation. The idea of a seeing a tattooed woman in a revealing bathing suit, in an era when bathing suits looked more like dressing gowns, drew many men into the tents of the sideshow – sometimes even accompanied by their wives or sweethearts.

Frances O'Connor was benefited from the innocent sexual undertones in her act. She was able to show a great deal of leg, more than was really appropriate in her prudish era, and she was never reprimanded for her actions. Frances showed her bare legs a lot – for they functioned as her arms.

Frances was born on September 8, 1914 in Renville County, Minnesota. Born without arms, she learned to use her feet in incredibly dexterous ways. Despite her physical condition, or perhaps because of it, Frances possessed a very outgoing personality. Combined with a natural beauty and the sheer spectacle her legs created as they competed otherwise mundane daily chores, made her a natural for the sideshow.

Her sideshow career began in Wyoming with the Al G. Barnes Circus – her mother serving as her manager – and eventually she worked with Ringling Bros. and Barnum & Bailey for over 20 years, until the mid 1940's. She was given the moniker of 'The Living Venus De Milo' and, while not the first sideshow worker given this name, she was perhaps the best suited. By all accounts she was a very beautiful woman who attracted droves of men and eligible suitors to her shows. Not only was she beautiful, but her sweet disposition made many men swoon and it had been said that she turned down hundreds of marriage proposals during her career.

Frances and her incredibly dexterous legs and feet were featured in the 1932 film *Freaks*. In the film, she did things such as smoking a cigarette, drinking from a cup, cutting her food with a fork and knife and using a napkin to dab the corners of her mouth – all performed with a ballerina-like grace. Francis was so capable with her feet that she was able to sew and knit as a hobby.

Eventually, as she aged, Francis lost interest in travelling and the crowds lost interest in her. Shortly after her mother passed away, she decided to completely retire from show business. Francis disappeared almost completely into obscurity overnight and, despite having many suitors in her prime, she never married or bore any children. She lived her remaining life alone in California before passing away in 1982 at the age of sixty-seven.

53 MATTHEW BUCHINGER

– The Little Man of Nuremberg

'The tricks he plays at cups and balls,
Tis wrong in any man, who calls,
Them slight of hand, as he gives out,
Their slight of stumps, and are no doubt ...
I'm sure that's the worst thing about his life,
That he had to suffer these terrible poems.'

– A handbill dating from 1726

Matthew Buchinger was born in Anspach, Germany in 1674 and was one of the most well-known performers of his day. He played over a dozen musical instruments, danced the hornpipe, and was an expert calligrapher, magician, and bowler. He built magnificent ships with bottles, and was a stunning marksman with a pistol. All of those accomplishments are even more impressive when you realise that he had no arms or legs and stood only 28 inches high.

His skills certainly seemed to impress ladies as he was married at least four times and fathered eleven children. There was a story that one of his wives was abusive and insulting – he put up with the behaviour until he simply snapped and he knocked her to the ground and thrashed her publicly. The event was immortalised in the form of a caricature published in the newspaper the following day.

During his lifetime, Buchinger performed for many kings – three successive kings of Germany – and several times before King George. He died in Cork, Ireland in 1732.

MYRTLE CORBIN

– The Four-Legged Woman

Myrtle Corbin, was known as the Four-Legged Woman, however that moniker was slightly misleading. While at a glance one could plainly see four legs dangling beyond the hem of her dress – only one pair belonged to her, the other set to her dipygus twin sister.

Born in Lincoln County, TN in 1868 and spending most of her childhood in Blount County, AL – where she could be found in the 1880 census – her condition was incredibly rare. The tiny body of her twin was only developed from the waist down and even then it was malformed – tiny and possessing only three toes on each foot. Myrtle was able to control the limbs of her sister but was unable to use them for walking and she herself had a difficult time getting around as she was born with a clubbed foot. Technically, the 'Four-Legged Woman' only had one good, usable leg.

Myrtle was a popular attraction with P.T. Barnum, and later with Ringling Bros. and Coney Island. Her popularity was likely linked to her showmanship – she would often dress the extra limbs with socks and shoes matching her own and this gave her a truly surreal appearance. Myrtle was so popular that she was able to earn as much as $450 dollars a week.

At the age of 19, Myrtle married a doctor named Clinton Bicknell. It was then that the other aspects of her bizarre anatomy became evident. It seemed that her twin sister was also fully sexually formed – thus Myrtle possessed two vaginas. She had four daughters and a son and it has been rumoured that three of her children were born from one set of organs and two from the other. Whether this is true or not; it is medically possible. In *Anomalies and Curiosities of Medicine* by George M. Gould and Walter L. Pyle, it was observed that both vaginas menstruated – thus indicating both were possibly sexually functional.

Myrtle passed on May 6, 1928, surrounded by family and friends.

PERUMAL

– The Happy Hindoo

Perumal was born in Madras, India in 1888 and his images are often mistaken for fellow multi-limbed Indian Laloo. Perumal began his exhibition career at a very young age and often appeared in photographs with a companion, Indian dwarf named Soopromanien, who was sometime mistakenly called Sami. Sami was Perumal's family name.

He toured primarily in Europe, but did tour briefly with the Ringling Bros. circus. While in America he gained a reputation for being a perfectionist and displayed a strong dislike for western culture. He often refused to eat 'American food' and eventually employed his own Indian cooks to prepare his meals.

Just like Laloo and other marvels with parasitic twin, Perumal's twin was billed as being female and was dressed accordingly. That was, of course impossible and all parasitic twins are same-sexed.

LEN AND ERNIE

– Two Boys with One Head

On July 7th, 1931 in Winnipeg, Manitoba, Ernie Defort was born with a parasitic twin attached to his sternum.

Ernie's brother consisted of a headless rudimentary body with two arms and two legs. As such, Erie was billed as 'Two Boys with One Head'. Ernie's twin was even given a name, and together they were often billed as 'Len and Ernie' or sometimes 'Lester and Ernie'. The body was actually quite well formed with two arms and legs

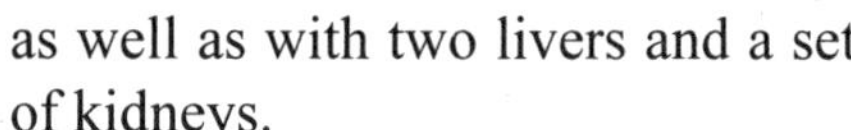

as well as with two livers and a set of kidneys.

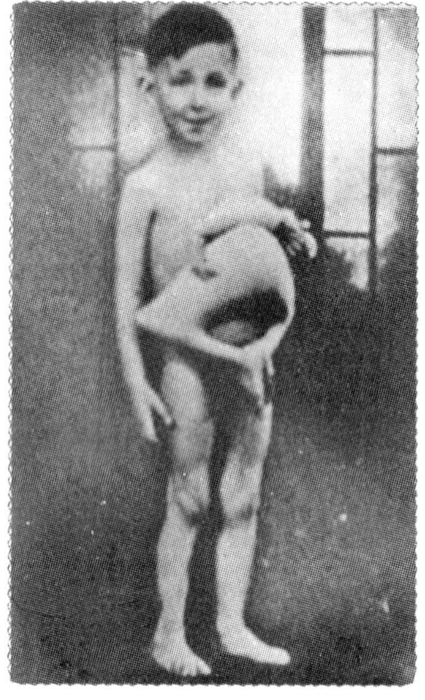

Ernie's short career was mostly limited to Canadian appearances with Conklin Shows. In 1942, Ernie's health began to be an issue due to the continued growth of his brother.

At the age of 12, the decision was made to amputate Len. Ernie was not pleased with the idea as he was very emotionally attached to his brother. He once was even quoted as saying that when spanked, he would prefer the bottom of his brother take the brunt.

He was taken to the famous Mayo Clinic in Rochester in December of 1943 where Len was amputated by renown surgeon and sarcoma specialist Dr. Henry Meyerding, known more for his cancer research then parasitic twin separation.

Dr. Meyerding observed that Ernie was an 'unusually strong and intelligent boy' stating that his intelligence at 12 was more on par with a 19-year-old. Furthermore, the Dr. claimed that Ernie would be ready to return to school 'in four to six weeks' after the operation.

Ernie physically survived the more than two hour operation and reportedly suffered depression and some psychological problems after the loss of the parasitic twin whom he regarded as a brother. However, he eventually came to terms with his loss and went on to live a full and well adjusted life, without the companionship of his 'little brother'.

Frank Conklin believes that Ernie was married later in life and would sometimes return to the Carnival later in life with his family.

••

FRANCESCO LENTINI

– The Three- Legged Man

Lentini was born in 1889 in Rosolini in the province of Sirocusa, Sicily as one of twelve children. Technically, he was one of 12 and a half children. His twin brother, who consisted of a leg and a set of genitals, was born attached to Francesco's spine. While he was billed as 'The Man With Three Legs', Lentini actually had four feet as a small malformed secondary foot protruded from his third leg. Thus in total he had three legs, four feet, sixteen toes and two sets of functioning male genitals. Furthermore, to complicate his life further, all of Francesco's legs were of different lengths.

As a child, Lentini hated his extra limbs and appendages. Doctors determined that because of their proximity to his spine, removal could have resulted in paralysis. Lentini was raised by his aunt after his parents refused to acknowledge him and she, meaning well, enrolled the young Lentini into a home for disabled children. While there he saw children far worse off than him. He saw children who could not walk at all and he gained a new appreciation for life. Lentini not only learned to walk, he also ran, jumped rope, rode a bicycle and even ice skate. His time at the home for disabled children was an experience he quoted for many years as his major motivation.

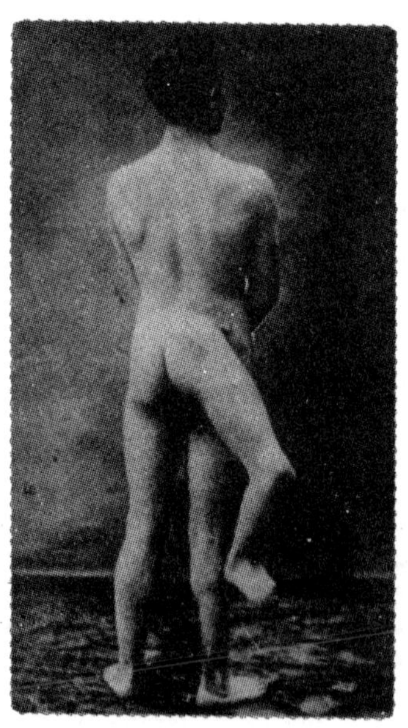

In 1898, at the age of eight, Lentini arrived in America and became an instant sensation. He charmed crowds with his keen wit and sense of humor. He wowed audiences with his unusual agility as well. He had amazing control over his extra appendage. During performances Lentini was well-known for kicking a soccer ball with the strange limb. As he grew older, Lentini's performances focused on his charming character.

He would conduct interviews while propped up on his extra limb, using it as a stool. He fielded questions ranging from his innocent hobbies to the particulars of his sex life. He was also often asked about his shoes. People wondered if it was difficult to buy shoes in a set of three. Showing his mental sharpness, he always revealed that he bought two pairs and gave the extra one to a one-legged friend.

His charm did not go unnoticed and a young lady named Theresa Murray soon took a liking to Lentini. The pair soon wedded and together they had four healthy children. Lentini continued touring until he died at the age of seventy-eight in 1966. His career spanned over forty years and he worked with every major circus and sideshow including Barnum & Bailey and Coney Island. Lentini was so respected among his peers that he was often simply called 'The King'.

GEORGE LIPPERT

– The Man with Three Legs and Two Hearts

George Lippert was born in Germany in 1844. In addition to being born with three legs, he was also born with two functioning hearts although that condition was unknown until his autopsy in 1906.

His third leg was fully formed and even possessed an extra toe, giving Lippert a total of sixteen. The leg was not functional. Lippert claimed that his leg had been fully functional until it sustained a fracture. Whether this was a fact or not remained a mystery, but during his career the leg hung motionless.

Early in his career, George was billed as the 'only Three Legged Man on Earth' and he proved to be quite an attraction. Lippert even worked as an exhibit with P. T. Barnum. However, evidence indicates that he may not have been the easiest person to do business with. No photographs exist of George Lippert. This pitch card shows only a painting of Lippert and remains the only pitch card ever used by Lippert. Considering that his career spanned decades and coincided with a great boom in sideshow photography, this is highly unusual and raises several red flags.

Furthermore, when another three legged man appeared in 1898, Lippert was quickly pushed aside and the new prodigy rose to great fame. The Three Legged Man was replaced. By 1899, Lippert was penniless and homeless. He eventually found a benefactor in a florist named Mary Riggs and Lippert with Riggs in Salem, Oregon for seven years.

In the summer of 1906, George Lippert died of tuberculosis at the age 62. The autopsy revealed his two hearts and also showed that one heart died two to three weeks before his eventual death. Doctors declared that if Lippert had not had tuberculosis he could have easily lived for many years. He would have been sustained by his secondary heart.

••

LALOO

– The Handsome, Healthy, Happy Hindoo

Laloo was born in Oudh, India as the second of the four siblings in 1874. He was accompanied into this world by his parasitic twin brother who was little more than a headless mass of limbs attached to his breastbone.

Laloo's brother consisted of two arms and two legs, a functioning penis with a complete urinary system and, although lacking testicles, the twin was quite capable of maintaining an erection at inopportune times. Unfortunately, the twin also needed to occasionally urinate and, although Laloo could detect tactile sensations through his brother, he was only aware of his brother's need to eliminate. Laloo took to diapering his sibling and, fortunately, the twin was unable to defecate.

Laloo was quite popular in nearly every big sideshow of his era, he travelled extensively and even worked with P. T. Barnum. His advertisements often billed him as the 'Handsome, Healthy, Happy Hindoo' – as exotic acts and persons were all the rage in America at that time. Also, in a bit of common showmanship, he would often dress his brother as a girl and advertise the twin as his sister. That was, until that erection issue started to throw a wrench into the act.

Laloo was also something of an rights activist and, in 1889, he participated in a well orchestrated protest to have sideshow performers referred to as 'prodigies' and not 'freaks'. The protest was successful and the word 'freak' fell out of common practice for quite some time.

By 1894 Laloo was married, to a average woman, and well off financially. Not only did he command great sums from his sideshow ventures, he also padded his income by offering to display his body to physicians for examinations at a great profit. It has been said that Laloo lived a very lavish lifestyle.

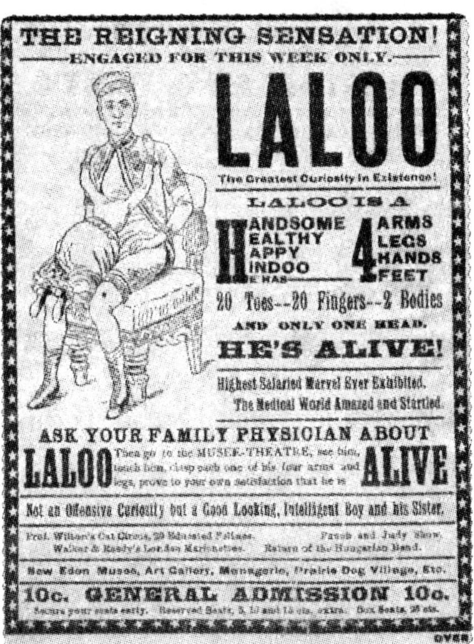

Unfortunately, Laloo died an early death in a train wreck in 1905 while working for the Norris and Rowe circus in Mexico.

BETTY LOU WILLIAMS

– Ripley's Four-Legged Wonder

At the 1934 World's Fair, Robert Ripley of the Ripley's 'Believe It Or Not' unveiled to the public his very first Odditorium. Previously, Ripley was known for his "Believe It Or Not" comic strip in newspapers. However, his World's Fair Odditorium featured real anatomical curiosities and the most spectacular of his presentations was an infant girl named Betty Lou Williams.

Betty Lou Williams was born Lillie B Williams in Albany, Georgia on January 10, 1932. She was the daughter of a poor farming family and the youngest of twelve children. She was also born attached at the side to a parasitic sibling that consisted of two legs, one tiny arm-like appendage and a more developed arm with three fingers. Despite the fact that the head of her twin was embedded deep within her abdomen, Betty Lou was a very healthy girl and doctors proclaimed that there was no reason she could not live a long and healthy life.

She was originally discovered at the age of one by a professional showman named Dick Best. Best changed the name of the little girl to Betty Lou – perhaps in an attempt to promote the parasite as a male, a lie that was popular in parasitic twin displays and he began to display the infant in his New York Museum. It was there that she drew the attention of Ripley.

Working for Ripley at the age of two, Betty Lou made an astounding $250 a week. As she grew into adulthood, she made over $1000 a week. With her earnings she purchased a 260 acre ranch for her parents and sent all eleven of her siblings to college.

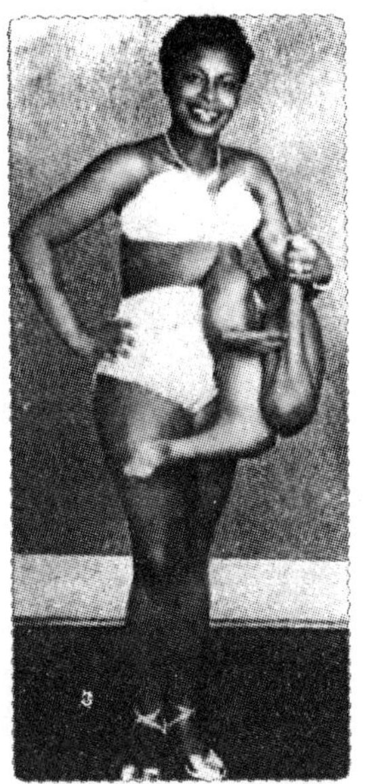

The jump in Betty Lou's earnings was due to the fact that she developed into quite an attractive woman as she matured. Her beauty and generosity drew many male suitors and, at the age of twenty-three, she became engaged to one of her admirers. However, the husband-to-be was little more than a heartbreaking thief. He left Betty Lou taking a great deal of money with him and, distraught over the breakup, Betty suffered a severe asthma attack at her home in Trenton, New Jersey. Betty Lou suffocated to death at the age of twenty-three.

••

61 JUAN BAPTISTA DOS SANTOS

– The Man with Two Swords

While there was scarce material on Blanche Dumas, her alleged lover Juan Baptista dos Santos was the subject of some fairly intense study.

Juan Baptista dos Santos was born in Portugal around 1843 in the town of Faro and was examined for the first time when he was only six months old. His parents and two siblings were well formed and it was said that his gestation and birth were uneventful. As a child, Juan was considered quite handsome, fit and well proportioned except for the two distinct genitalia and extra fused limbs he possessed.

It was observed that urination proceeded simultaneously from both penises. What appeared to be a third leg dangling from the pubis was in fact two limbs fused together as one with a small

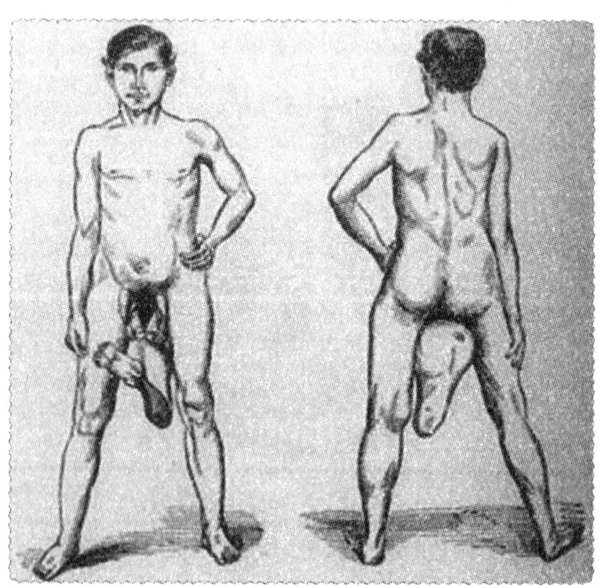

and supernumerary anus. The compound limb had a patella but, while the limb joint was freely movable, it had no motor control or power of motion. A journal, published in London states that Juan Baptista dos Santos had been exhibited in Paris, and that the surgeons advised operation.

That operation never occurred as a further report from Havana, dated July, 1865, details a further detailed examination of Santos at twenty-two years of age. This report also brought forward the claim that Santos possessed an 'animal passion' and had a ravenous sexual appetite and permissive reputation. This same report claimed that Juan Baptista dos Santos used both penises during intercourse and, after finishing with one he would continue with the other.

A further report gave details of the physiology of Santos in full adulthood and was accompanied by a detailed illustration. This report also detailed Santos was in the habit of wearing this limb in a special sling or bound firmly to his right thigh. This not only prevented the limb from dangling, it also allowed him greater freedom of activity – he was said to be an avid horseback rider.

During his lifetime, Santos was perused by several sideshows and circuses. In 1865, he turned down a contract worth 200,000 francs to perform in a French circus. However, Santos opted to exhibit himself to medical authorities and rare 'special' exhibitions. Despite his extensive medical examinations and relative fame in medial circles only one photo of Juan Baptista dos Santos was found and that focuses mainly on his dual genitalia.

62 BLANCHE DUMAS

– The Three-Legged Courtesan

It is believed that Blanche Dumas was born on the island of Martinique in 1860 to a French father and a mother who was a quadroon (one quarter black). At the age of 25, Blanche was visited and documented by Bechlinger of Para, Brazil and consequently added to the pages of *Anomalies and Curiosities of Medicine.* According to *Anomalies and Curiosities of Medicine,* Blanche had a 'modified duplication of the lower body'.

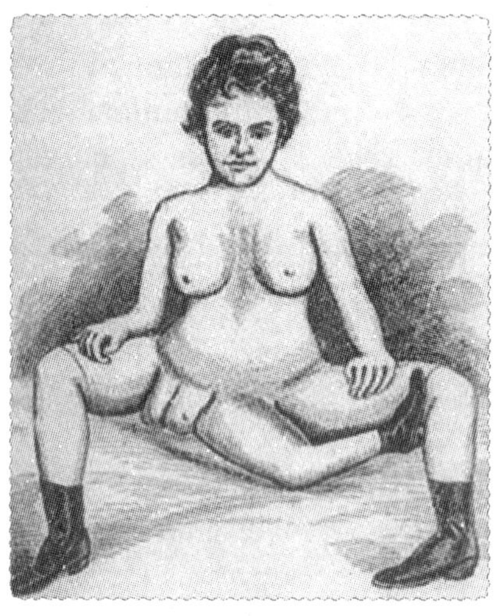

She purportedly had a very broad pelvis, two imperfectly developed legs and a third leg attached to her coccygeus and, in addition to normal well developed breasts, she also had two smaller rudimentary breasts – complete with nipples – close together above her pubic area. Furthermore, Blanche also had two vaginas and two well-developed vulvas and both had equally developed sensitivity. Her sexual appetite was said to be very pronounced. She was known to have many male admirers and was known to entertain men with both her vaginas.

So pronounced was Blanche's libido that she eventually moved to Paris and became a courtesan. Also, upon hearing stories that a three legged man with dual genitalia named Juan Baptista dos Santos was in Paris on a European tour, she expressed a sincere desire to have sex with him. While there was no evidence that the two had illicit meetings but there wass great rumour of a brief affair.

MAXIMO & BARTOLA

– The Aztec Children

Maximo and Bartola first appeared in 1848 and the hoax perpetrated by their handler in the spirit of shameless promotion not only sustained their long careers, but also the careers of two generations to come.

Maximo and Bartola were born microcephalic and were originally from the village of Decora in St. Salvador. The pair were quite intellectually slow and required special care. Their mother, Marina Espina was conned into handing her unique children over to a Spanish trader named Ramon Selva. Ramon promised to take the pinheaded children to America, he assured Marina that they would be cured of their condition. Instead, Ramon sold Maximo and Bartola to an American promoter named Morris.

Morris concocted an incredible story to introduce the children to the American public.

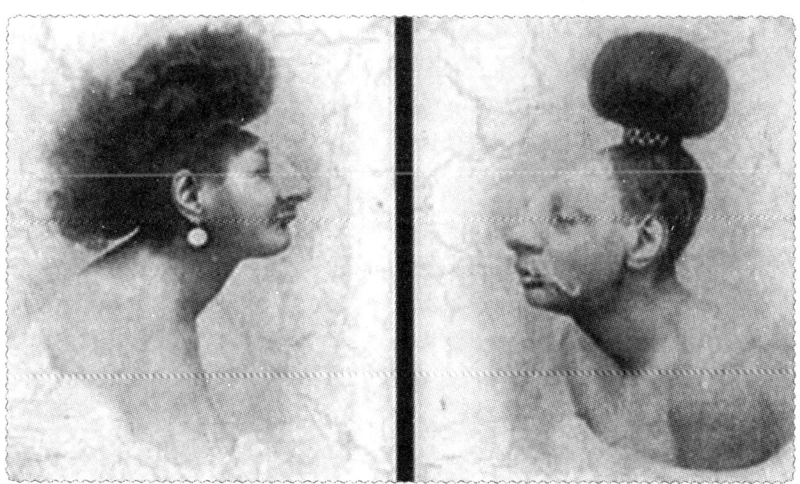

At the time America was frothing around the display of 'ethnological curiosities'. Interest in the Mayan civilisation was peaking due to recent explorations and publications. Morris sold a forty-eight page booklet in conjunction with his exhibiting of Maximo and Bartola to capitalise on the recent appetite of the public. Life of the living Aztec children told the elaborate 'true story' surrounding the discovery of Maximo and Bartola in an Aztec temple in a lost city.

The booklet alleged that Maximo and Bartola were found squatting on alters and that they were members of a sacred race once worshipped by the city's inhabitants. To further this claim, Morris dressed the pair in Aztec-looking garb. Both wore costumes featuring Aztec suns sewn onto the front and their hair was allowed to grow bushy. This combined with their diminutive stature and proportionately small heads did give them a highly unusual appearance. But would the public believe they were members of a lost race?

Rather than scoff at these wild claims, the public actually believed the pitch. To those who viewed them, Maximo and Bartola were the last remnants of an ancient civilisation.

Not only did the public show a great amount of interest, the scientific community clamoured for a chance to examine the Aztec children. Numerous papers were published on the topic of Maximo and Bartola including the American Journal of Medical Sciences. Soon Maximo and Bartola were the darlings of the general public and high society. Eventually, they visited the White House as guests of President Fillmore.

In 1853 Morris took Maximo and Bartola to England. There they were exhibited before the Ethnological Society and summoned to Buckingham Palace. During their public exhibition in London, they attracted three thousand people in just two days. Anatomist Prof. Richard Owen visited Maximo and Bartola and soon he and the rest of the European scientific community were debating exactly what the Aztec children were and these debates further fuelled their popularity. During their subsequent tour of Europe, they appeared before Napoleon and his imperial family, the emperor of Russia, the emperor of Austria as well as the kings and queens of Bavaria, Holland and Belgium. Everywhere Maximo and Bartola went, controversy and conjecture followed. To many, they were indeed examples of an unknown race of people; they were the last of the Aztec children.

Maximo and Bartola eventually returned to the United States, this time for exhibition at Barnum's American Museum. Barnum renamed the duo as 'The Aztec Wonders' and many of the photos that exist of Maximo and Bartola are from this era of their career. Eventually interest in the pair died down as reporters and the scientific community moved on to other more legitimate discoveries. In an attempt to rekindle public interest, they resurfaced on January 7, 1867 in London and appeared to marry each other. They were married under the names of Senior Maximo Valdez Nunez and Senora Bartola Velasquez and, despite being brother and sister, it was alleged that by 'Aztec Culture' such a marriage was allowed. The publicity attempt was a complete failure and nor was an eyebrow raised.

It is alleged that Maximo and Bartola continued to be exhibited until 1901 under the care of several different managers; the details of their eventual end are unknown.

••

ZIP

– The Pinhead

A pinhead is a person born with a condition known as microcephaly. It is a neurological disorder and is characterised by a smaller than average head. Biologically, during conception the head fails to grow in time with the face which continues to develop at a normal rate; this produces a person with a small head and a receding forehead. As the individual grows older, the smallness of the skull becomes more obvious, although the entire body also is often underweight and dwarfed. It is very common that the development of motor functions and speech are also usually delayed and mental retardation is common in persons with microcephaly. The term microcephaly is really a blanket term for many similar disorders. It may be congenital or the result of various syndromes associated with chromosomal abnormalities. What is known is that pinheads have always been a very popular draw.

Most pinheads are shorter than average and have a very distinct appearance thus, during the early years of sideshow, many pinheads were exhibited as a variant species – The Missing Link or The Last of the Aztecs were common monikers. There was one individual during the Golden Age of sideshow who was simply considered indescribable. Those who looked upon Zip – the Pinhead simply had to exclaim, 'What is it?'

Born in 1842 as William Henry Johnson, Zip was technically a pinhead, however his condition was not nearly as pronounced as many of the other pinhead performers. However, he enjoyed an incredibly long and profitable career and over those many years he was known by many names. At various stages in his career he was 'The Monkey Man' or 'The Man-Monkey'. He was also known as 'The Missing Link' and 'Zip, the Pinhead'.

While William was actually born in New Jersey, those who saw him on stage would swear that he was from another planet. When P. T. Barnum recruited him in 1860 and transformed him into Zip.

Barnum shaved William's head except for a small tuft on the top of his head and dressed him in a bizarre fur suit and then pitched Zip as a missing link. Barnum claimed that Zip was found during a gorilla-hunting expedition near the Gambia River in western Africa and he also claimed that Zip was the member of a 'naked race of men, travelling about by climbing on tree branches'.

Zip dove into his character. He would never speak during a performance and would only grunt when addressed or questioned. Legend actually has it that Barnum paid Zip a dollar every day to keep quiet and in character. By all accounts Zip earned that dollar by acting like a complete and total madman.

Charles Dickens visited and attended a performance by Zip in 1867 as a personal guest of P. T. Barnum. As he watched Zip on stage behaving like a lunatic with his pointed head, asked Barnum quite seriously, 'Barnum, what is it?' Barnum was ecstatic at this reaction and repeated the 'What is it' phrase on posters, pamphlets and billboards so extensively that for a time many people thought the character William portrayed was actually named 'What is it', and not Zip at all. Regardless of the confusion, Zip became Barnum's most consistent draw and due to that position Zip became one of the better paid performers – $100 a week in addition to that $1 a day 'hush money'.

Zip outlasted Barnum's solo ventures and continued to work with Ringling Bros. and Barnum and Bailey shows. He was often featured at Coney Island and in dime museums across the U.S. William's character gradually evolved considerably from the wildman persona and into more of a comedy act. Zip would carry around a pop gun and fired it off at other performers who threatened his popularity and he later took to playing violin enthusiastically and so poorly that patrons would pay him to stop. It was also during that time that Zip assumed another nickname; he was known as 'The Playful Pinhead'. During that time he was very well-known for his comic behaviour. When patrons tossed coins onto the stage – as was common at the time – Zip would scurry about and toss the coins back, as if insulted by having someone throw something at him. As a publicity stunt, he came forward during the Scope monkey trial of 1925 and offered himself as evidence.

As he became older and a senior member of the sideshow community, Zip came to be known as the 'Dean of Freaks' and he continued to perform into his 80's until he passed on April 24, 1926 of bronchitis. His funeral was attended by hundreds of fellow performers as he was loved and respected by his peers. The funeral home on that day was filled to capacity with his fellow freak performers – all paying their last respects to the greatest marvel of the era. The funeral must have been quite the sight as mourners included giants like Jim Tarver, the Texas Giant and Jack Earle, the Tallest Man in the World and Fat Ladies, like Jolly Irene, who required entire pews just to be seated. Other marvelous mourners were not as easily identifiable as Frank Graf, the Tattooed Man wore a modest suit and Joe Kramer, the man with the rubber neck, stood facing forward for a change. Many other human wonders attended the service – from sword swallowers to midgets- and all of them had known Zip for many years.

But there is a lot of speculation as to how well anyone knew Zip. There are a number of questions in regards to the true level of intelligence. Most pinheads suffer from serious mental retardation. However, many of the things Zip did during his lifetime hints that he was highly intelligent. First, and perhaps the most convincing, he maintained his public character 24 hours a day for 66 years. In 1925, Zip became a real hero as he saved the life of a drowning woman during a break from a Coney Island Dime Museum.

His manager through much of his career, Captain O. K. White, helped him save money and Zip died a wealthy man. He owned several houses – one was a gift from Barnum. He left his fortune to his beloved sister and died a famous icon that continues to live on. His manager Captain White claimed that he never saw Zip unhappy except when he wasn't on tour. 'He amuses the crowd and the crowd amuses him,' White once said.

Finally, rumour has it that on his deathbed, his final words to his sister were, "Well, we fooled 'em for a long time."

●●

NICCOLO PAGANINI

– The Devil's Violinist

Niccolò Paganini, born October 27, 1782, was and still is considered by many as the greatest violin virtuosi to have ever lived. While the 19th century saw several extraordinary violinists, the Italian Paganini was so beyond his peers that it was rumoured by his contemporaries that he had sold his soul to the devil.

Paganini first learned to play the mandolin from his father at the age of five before moving on to the violin. He began composing at seven and, by the age of twelve, he was performing publicly. At the age of sixteen, Paganini had a breakdown of sorts and disappeared into alcoholism. Eventually, with the aid of an unnamed female benefactor, he managed to quit drinking. Once sober, he sequestered himself away for three years and studied the violin obsessively. When he returned to the public eye at the age of twenty-two, he became the first music superstar.

Paganini was capable of playing three octaves across four strings in a hand span, a nearly impossible feat, even by today's standards. His flexibility and exceptionally long fingers have resulted in speculation that he may have had Marfan syndrome, a genetic mutation not identified until 1899 that results in elongated fingers and other unique traits. Others have conjectured that he had Ehlers-Danlos syndrome, commonly know as Rubber Man Syndrome, and still other attribute his abilities to his instrument.

In the early 1830's, Paganini's health began to deteriorate rapidly. And in 1834, he no longer had the stamina to play his violin and he retired from public performance. The great violinist to ever live died in Nice on May 27, 1840.

SUSI
– The Elephant Girl

Ichthyosis finds its etymological origins in the Greek term for 'fish', however the majority of human exhibits afflicted with the skin condition often adopted an alligator-themed epithet. Susi's skin, however, was particularly coarse and cracked and the title of 'elephant-skinned' seemed more appropriate and illustrative.

While accounts do vary, Susi was likely born in 1909 as Charlotte in the western district of Berlin. In early childhood, Susi's ichthyosis manifested aggressively and her skin quickly thickened, turned grey and cracked to visually elephantine properties. Due to the severity of her condition, Susi endured daily physical pain. Her pain was further amplified by multiple infections and illnesses as bacteria invaded the major cracks formed in her skin from even her most subtle movements. During her early years, Susi couldn't even blink her eyes without risking life-threatening cracks.

In addition to the physical pain, Susi also endured emotional pain as she was the subject of ridicule and segregation from her peers. During the hot summer days, while the other children frolicked in the water, Susi rubbed ice over her arms in an effort to cool down as her skin condition left her unable to sweat. As the children pointed and laughed at her, she would not shed a single tear. Her condition had robbed her of that ability as well.

Susi's parents, in an effort to improve the quality of her life and to prevent infection opportunities, lathered Susi with generous amounts of oil and moisturiser on a daily basis. Susi's parents were also highly concerned with her general appearance and took to peeling the skin from her face on a nightly basis. Both practices did wonders as her skin became suppler and her facial complexion cleared to reveal an attractive face. Susi would, however, need to repeat the daily procedures for the rest of her life.

Susi first came to the United States in 1927 as part of a troupe consisting of a giantess and a bearded lady and she made multiple subsequent visits to the U.S. With her manager, she emigrated to the U.S. from Germany to escape the oncoming war and moved into an apartment on New York's west side. While living in New York, Susi often exhibited herself at Hubert's Museum on 42nd Street and Coney Island in the 1930's. She even worked at Madison Square Garden for the Ringling show in 1967.

By all accounts Susi was a shy, introvert and quiet woman who preferred to keep a low profile and exhibit sparingly. She exhibited herself more or less locally until her manager passed away in the late 1960's. With his death, Susi's career and heart for the business died as well. Her last confirmed public appearance was at the Great Allentown Fair in Pennsylvania as a single attraction billed as 'The Swamp Girl'.

By some accounts Susi retired to Germany, but most report that she passed away in New York City in 1975.

67 COUNT ORLOFF

– The Transparent Man

Few human wonders can ever compare to the unusual case of Count Orloff. He was a human oddity sometimes incorrectly billed as ossified, and correctly touted as being transparent.

Ivannow Wladislaus von Dziarski-Orloff was born in Hungary in 1864. While he was completely normal during his childhood, at the age of 14 he began to experience an unknown wasting disease. By early adulthood, Orloff was little more than a living skeleton – unable to stand and in constant pain. To deal with his tragic pain, Orloff took to the opium pipe – strangely enough the pipe became something of a trademark as many of his pitch cards pictured him puffing away and 'chasing the dragon'.

While during his career, Orloff was known as an ossified man, his condition was actually quite the opposite. Orloff actually had a lack of bone density and this allowed his bones to bend and twist. Furthermore, his skin was paper thin and his musculature so atrophied that, with the aid of a bright spotlight, spectators could actually see the blood coursing through his veins. Not only that, but when a bright light was placed behind Orloff, the warm glow could actually been seen from the other side.

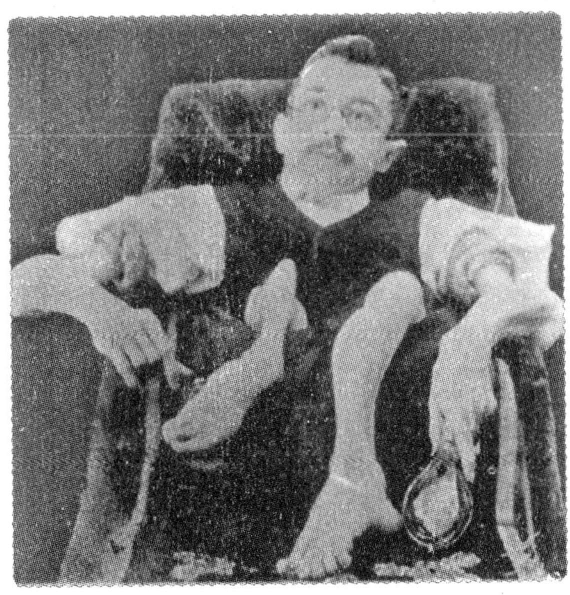

As strange as Orloff was – many promoters felt a need to further embellish it. As a result – to this day, some still claim that a person could read a newspaper through the body of Orloff. A claim made in an early pamphlet.

Orloff was known primarily as the Living Ossified and Transparent Man, but later in life he adopted the moniker of 'The Human Window Pane'. His tendency to show himself as a medical specimen allowed him to travel around the world. Eventually he went into business for himself – he owned his own successful sideshow. Orloff died in 1904.

68 JOHN HOLTUM

– The Cannonball Man

At one point in history every circus, carnival, and vaudeville hall had a strongman on hand to astound spectators. The image of a mustachioed man clad in leopard print while hoisting a bending barbell high aloft is still synonymous with circuses. The spectacles these men provided ranged from the highly impressive to the borderline mundane but in a golden age populated with hundreds of contemporaries, an individual simply had to go the extra mile to ensure fame and fortune.

John Holtum elected to stand apart by becoming a human target. Holtum caught cannonballs fired directly at his him from point-blank range.

Born on October 29, 1845 in the Danish town of Haderslev, John Holtum led a relatively uneventful life until finally enlisting as a sailor at fifteen. His work on deck and in shipyards sculpted the muscular physique he would eventually be known for. In time, Holtum found his way to California and after a string of temporary heavy manual labour jobs, he found work in San Francisco as a professional strongman. There, he learnt and practised the basic feats most strongmen mongered.

It wasn't until Holtum returned to Europe in 1870 that he stuck upon the idea of catching a cannonball.

The experts Holtum asked told him it couldn't be done and his initial attempts seemed to support those claims and his experiments almost took his life. One failed attempt saw Holtum purportedly loose a couple of fingers. After two years of training and against all odds Holtum perfected the feat, and from then on his fortune and reputation were made.

It was a feat that required immense strength, steely nerves and lightning fast reflexes. It was a feat that never failed to stun witnesses. An assistant would load the cannonball into a regulation cannon on one side of the stage and after a deafening explosion the ball would fly directly toward Holtum. Wearing only a pair of sturdy gloves and a pad on his chest for minimal protection, Holtum would attempt to catch the speeding projectile with his hands. As soon as Holtum caught the cannonball, he would throw it quickly to the ground. He knew that the ball would burn his flesh if not released immediately.

Was there trickery involved? Perhaps so. Perhaps the charge of gunpowder was much less than what would have been used in battle. Perhaps the ball was lighter or perhaps it was completely hollow. Such claims were made by the public, however Holtum offered 3000 francs to anyone who could perform a similar feat and no one ever took up the challenge. The stunt was death-defying and only Holtum dared to face the Grim Reaper.

The Danish-born strongman continued to draw crowds wherever he performed and his fame continued to grow. His charm, his physique and his death-defying ways made Holtum something of sex-symbol. In Paris, a group of female fans petitioned to ban his performance. They feared that their Adonis would meet an early demise – or worse – that his beautiful body would be maimed.

Eventually, Holtum decided to retire. He married a pretty equestrienne and settled down in England where he lived in considerable comfort until he died peacefully in 1919.

••

SANDWINA

– Woman of Steel

The story of iron-strong women, the beguiling Charmion and the mighty Minerva is well-known. However, one name that should never be omitted from the records of curious history is Sandwina, a woman who at her peak was perhaps the most physically powerful person walking the planet earth.

The mighty Sandwina was born as Kate Brumbach in 1884 in Vienna, Austria to Bavarian parents. Her parents were circus strength performers of rather hearty proportions in their own right. Her father Philippe was said to possess a barrel chest of 56 inches and her mother Johanna had muscle laden biceps measuring over 15 inches. Together the pair of prodigious physical prodigies sired fourteen children.

Kate's three sisters, Barbara, Eugenia and Marie possessed great physical strength and performed alongside their parents in power demonstrations. Kate, however, was gifted with strength unparalleled to her siblings and was the only one to go on to spectacular fame.

Kate's natural strength came from her lineage and physical proportions. In adolescence Kate stood just over six feet tall and weighed 187 pounds. She honed her natural abilities through intensive exercise and in her heyday, she was known for her bulging 17 inch biceps and 26 ½ inch thighs. Kate initially displayed her muscular girth to the paying patrons of the circuses her father contracted with. She initially wrestled with men and famously offered 100 marks to any man who could beat her. According to legend, she never lost her bet and even gained a husband after soundly thrashing a young man by the name of Max Heymann. Heymann thought tussling with a woman would be a rather delightful way to earn 100 marks. But by his own account, he recalled only entering the ring, a blue sky and being carried away from the ring by Kate like a prize. The couple remained married for 52 years.

Kate appeared on the world stage quite suddenly while visiting New York. In a promotional stunt and after boasting of her strength, Kate made an open challenge daring anyone to lift more weight than she. To her surprise, and to the surprise of those assembled, none other than the father of powerlifting and bodybuilding Eugen Sandow took Kate up on her challenge.

Sandow was a man carved of granite. Indeed, he had sculpted his body to resemble the statues of the old Gods he saw as a child. He was considered the most physically gifted man in the world and Kate was certain that she had made a grave error in judgement. Still the contest began as Kate began lifting increasingly heavy weights and Sandow, subsequently, lifted those she was done with. This went on for some time, until Kate hoisted the unholy sum of 300 pounds above her head with one hand. Sandow could only raise the weight to his chest and Kate was declared the winner. It was shortly thereafter that Kate adopted the name Sandwina – a feminine derivative of 'Sandow' – though it was unclear if this action was a tribute or a taunt.

From then on Sandwina was known exclusively for her feats of strength. She was known to routinely juggle 30 pound iron spheres and press her 165 pound husband above her head using one arm. Some of her more famous feats involved lifting horses, maintaining carousels of 14 persons on her shoulders and carrying a half ton of cannons on her back. In between all of that, she also bore a son, Theodore Sandwina.

Sandwina did the bulk of her touring in the United States and was still performing with the Ringling Bros. and Barnum and Bailey Circus at the age of 57 in 1941. At the age of 64, Sandwina retired from touring and opened a restaurant with her husband in

New York. On occasion she was still known to delight patrons by breaking horseshoes, bending steel bars and on the rare occurrence by hoisting her husband skyward. Her son, Theodore had inherited his mother's formable strength and grew to 6 foot 2 inches and 200 pounds. He used his impressive strength and size to become a champion boxer and retired with a record of 46 wins – 38 of those by knockout.

On January 21, 1952, Sandwina lost her first and only wrestling bout to cancer. While cancer won and claimed her life, it could not take away her mark on history or her title of Strongest Woman in the World.

••

70 EUGEN SANDOW

– Father of Bodybuilding

In the Victorian era, Eugen Sandow must have physically appeared godly. While professional strongmen existed long before Sandow appeared, none possessed such a chiselled physique previously.

He was born Friederich Wilhelm Mueller in Konigsberg, Prussia in 1867, what is today Kaliningrad, Russia. By the time he was nineteen, Sandow was already performing strongman stunts in various sideshows. He was initially known for his impressive barbell routines and for breaking a chain locked around his chest. However, audiences quickly became far more fascinated by Eugen Sandow's bulging muscles than by the amount of weight he was able to hoist. As a result, Sandow developed and performed poses. He dubbed these displays as 'muscle display performances' and the routine was a precursor to the bodybuilding competition possess today. His routines and physique quickly made Sandow a sensation and a highly sought after carnival attraction.

Sandow was compared to a Roman God. His resemblance to the physiques of classic Greek and Roman sculpture was no accident. Sandow had visited Italy as a child and it was there, after gazing and admiring the bulging physiques of the ancient Gods, that his passion for sculpting his body took root. In training, Sandow actually measured the marble artworks in museums. He viewed them as 'The Grecian Ideal' and as a formula for the 'perfect physique'.

Sandow eventually built his physique to the exact proportions of Greek and Roman Sculpture and in the process, became one of the first athletes to intentionally develop his musculature to pre-determined dimensions. Today, he is considered by many to be 'The Father of Bodybuilding'.

Sandow performed all over Europe, and went to America to perform at the 1893 World's Columbian Exposition in Chicago. There he could be seen in a black velvet-lined box with his body covered in white powder to appear even more like a marble statue come to life. His popularity grew due to his cultured appearance, high intelligence, and well-mannered disposition. He also dressed very well and had a charming European accent, coupled with deep blue eyes and hearty laugh. He was befriended by the likes of King George V of the United Kingdom, Thomas Edison and Sir Arthur Conan Doyle. He eventually married Blanche Brooks Sandow and had two daughters. But he was constantly in the company of other women who actually paid money to feel his flexed muscles after his stage performances. Sandow also had a close relationship with a male musician and composer he hired to accompany him during his shows. The degree of their relationship had never been determined, but they lived together in New York for some time. It was clear that Blanche was jealous of his relationships.

Sandow was also a very astute businessman. He authored five books, owned a mail-order physical instruction and exercise equipment business and was the inventor of a unique spring-loaded dumbbell and a weighted rubber band resistance training system. Sandow's fame was instrumental in popularising home training equipment. Sandow also produced and promoted *Sandow Cigars*, *Sandow's Health & Strength Cocoa* and *Sandow*, a magazine devoted to physical culture. He opened a physical culture studio in London, one of the first health clubs to contrast starkly with the 'sweaty' gymnasiums that had already existed, and he made exercise fashionable for all classes. Sandow organised the first ever bodybuilding contest on September 14, 1901 called the 'Great Competition' and held it in the Royal Albert Hall, London, UK. The event was judged by himself, Sir Charles Lawes, and Sir Arthur

Conan Doyle; the contest was a huge success and was a sell-out with hundreds of fans turned away.

At the time of his death in 1925, a cover story was released stating Sandow died prematurely at age 58 of a stroke shortly after pushing his car out of the mud. The actual cause of death was more likely due to complications from syphilis. Sandow was buried in an unmarked grave at the request of his wife, Blanche (who never divorced him) at Putney Vale Cemetery near London. In 2002, a gravestone and black marble plaque was added by Sandow admirer and author Thomas Manly. The gold-lettered inscription reads – Eugen Sandow, 1867-1925, the Father of Bodybuilding.

Since 1977, as recognition of his contribution to the sport of bodybuilding, a bronze statue of Sandow has been presented to Mr Olympia winners. The statue is simply known as 'The Sandow'.

••

71 MINERVA & CHARMION

– Strong Women

The strongman has long been a staple in circus and sideshows. The image of handlebar mustached man garbed in a leopard print leotard has become the stereotypical image associated with feats of extraordinary strength. But, what about the 'fairer sex'? Was there ever a professional strong woman? Truth be told, there were several. Perhaps the best known and traditional of these brawny babes was Josephine Blatt, who was better known by her stage name Minerva.

Josephine Blatt's early history is shrouded in carnival gimmickry. She claimed to have been born in 1865 in Hamburg Germany but other sources, most notably The Guinness Book of World Records, pegged her as an American born in 1867 in Hoboken, New Jersey. Regardless of this discrepancy, few questions exist in regards to her remarkable strength.

In her displays, she demonstrated her strength by breaking horseshoes with her hands, breaking steel chains by expanding her chest, and playing catch with a 24 pound cannonball. She was capable to lift a stone weight of 360 lbs with a single finger thrust through a lifting ring. Furthermore, The Guinness Book of Records recognised Minerva as having lifted the greatest weight ever by a woman. At the Bijou Theatre in Hoboken on April 15, 1895, Josephine Blatt lifted 3,564 lbs in a hip-and-harness lift. With that superhuman lift, Josephine Blatt nearly achieved the mythical status of her namesake.

She retired with her strongman husband, Charles Blatt, in 1910 and eventually passed away on September 1, 1923.

Around the same time when Minerva was raising great weights, a young lady named Charmion was raising eyebrows with her unusual strength-related act.

Laverie Vallee was a Sacramento born trapeze artist who possessed strength and a physique most men would be envious of. However, she was most well-known for her risqué striptease performances.

The act opened with Charmion taking the stage in full Victorian attire. She would then mount the trapeze and proceed to undress to her leotard while performing impressive and strength-dependant stunts. The act was incredibly impressive and provocative for the era. However, the controversy created by her performances did not prevent the formulation of a devoted, and mostly male fan base.

One of her greatest fans was Thomas Edison. As a result of that adoration, on November 11, 1901 Charmion committed a simplified version of her act to film for Edison. The film, simply entitled *Trapeze Disrobing Act* focused more on the erotic aspect of the performance, though a few remarkable feats of strength are featured.

Charmion eventually retired to Santa Ana, California. She passed away on February 6, 1949 at the age of 73.

••

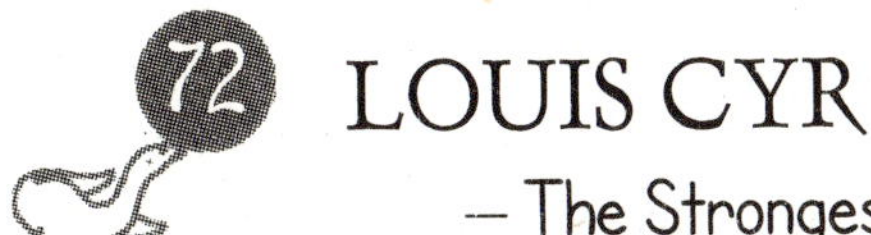

LOUIS CYR

– The Strongest Man in History

Not all human wonders are unique in appearance. Many are unique in their deeds. Some of the most unfathomable deeds and physical feats were performed by the strongmen of sideshow. Perhaps the most famous of these strongmen was the Canadian Colossus Louis Cyr.

Louis Cyr was born Cyprien-Noé Cyr on October 10, 1863 in the Quebec town of St. Cyprien de Napierville. Louis was a large child, weighing close to 18 pounds at birth and from an early age, those around him were impressed with his natural strength. At the age of twelve, Louis was a lumberjack and stories of his strength became legendary amongst his peers and co-workers. In 1878, at the age of seventeen, Louis and his family immigrated to the United States. Standing just five feet and ten inches but weighing over 230 pounds, Louis presented his first public display of strength in Boston during a strongest man competition. He stunned the crowd by lifting a horse clear off the ground.

Attempting to capitalise on his stunning performance, Louis returned to Quebec in 1882 and went on a brief tour of Quebec with his wife and family as 'The Troupe Cyr'. At the conclusion of his tour, Louis became a police officer in Montreal.

Restless in his vocation, he entered another strongman competition in March of 1886 hosted by Quebec City. His competition was with the World's Strongest Man, David Michaud. During the competition, Louis lifted a 218 pound barbell with one hand. The best Michaud could manage was 158 pounds. Louis also amazed his opponent by squatting a platform weighing 2,371 pounds. Louis was then 'officially' the strongest man in the world.

It is important to note that the physical feats performed by strongmen are often exaggerated and Louis was no exception to this rule. There are stories surrounding Louis that border on the impossible.

However, many of his feats were formally documented by witnesses and officials. While touring the world, Louis once squatted a platform holding 18 men. He also lifted a 500 pound weight with one finger and, in a stunning publicity stunt, pushed a freight car up an incline. His greatest feat of all occurred on October 12, 1891, in Montreal. On that occasion, he legitimately won a tug-of-war against four horses.

Although Louis Cyr died of chronic nephritis on November 10, 1912, his legacy lives on. He was dubbed 'The Strongest Man in History' for his amazing physical strength and today there is a district of Montreal named Louis-Cyr in his honour. It is located in Saint-Henri – the same area he patrolled as a police officer. There is also a park, the Parc Louis-Cyr, named after Louis and a statue of 'The Strongest Man in History' has stood in the Place des Hommes-Forts, 'Strongman's Square' since 1970.

The cause of his herculean strength is still unknown but during his remarkable lifetime, Louis never backed down from a challenge and he was undefeated in Canada and abroad.

HADJI ALI

– The Great Regurgitator

The Great Regurgitator, who was also billed as The Egyptian Enigma, was born Hadji Ali in Egypt in 1892. In the 1920's, Hadji Ali came to be something of an American vaudeville sensation for his unusual ability to swallow unique items, regurgitate them in an order specific to audience requests and for his 'human water spout' routine.

Professional regurgitation and the human water spout acts were actually nothing new. In the mid 17th century, a Frenchman named Jean Royer was known for his regurgitating and spouting abilities. Another spouter, Blaise Manfre was noted for his ability to drink water and regurgitate wine. Of course, his feat was accomplished by simply swallowing Brazil wood extract before the water which would then tint the liquid deep red. The regurgitation act was also common enough for Houdini to make mention of it, and his distaste for the act, in his book *Miracle Mongers and Their Methods*.

There was really no trick to the regurgitator act as it was a matter of controlled vomiting and repetitive training of the muscles of the stomach and throat to clench at will. Some performers were known to use substances to induce violent stomach spasms while retaining firm lip control, but those individuals who lacked poise and presence, their careers were short lived.

Ali brought a lot of unique elements to an act that had been virtually forgotten. His rather unique and foreign appearance certainly captured attention as did the vast amounts of water he was able to ingest and expel with ferocious pinpoint precision. Ali was known to swallow two or three fishbowls of water, cup by cup, and eject a six foot arc into a small waiting basin. Ali was able to accomplish the same feat even after swallowing numerous items before ingesting the water, displaying some ability to compartmentalise his stomach.

In his finale, as drums roared and his assistant erected a small metal castle on stage, Ali would down a gallon of water followed by a gallon of kerosene. Expelling the kerosene in a powerful jet, Ali would ignite the castle in flames, feed the flames with subsequent gusts, and then extinguish the inferno by driving out the water he had swallowed previously. He performed his act a minimum of twenty-two times a week.

While other regurgitators were present in Ali's era, like Harry, The Human Hydrant and Morton, The Great Waldo, their acts failed to really catch on. Morton's act consisted primarily of downing mugs of beer on stage and regurgitating them before he became intoxicated and came across as being rather lowbrow while Waldo's incorporation of living mice and rats terrified onlookers. The mere fact the Ali's vomiting was regarded as impressive and credible entertainment certainly shows that his presentation and showmanship was remarkable.

Thankfully, Hadji Ali's act was immortalised in the Laurel and Hardy movie *Politiquerias*, a Spanish-language version of the Laurel and Hardy movie *Chicken comes Home* and he also appeared in a contemporary documentary called *Gizmo*.

While touring England and still enjoying a wave of unexpected popularity, Hadji Ali died of heart failure on November 5, 1937 in Staffordshire, England. The tradition of professional regurgitating has since been carried on by UK native Stevie Starr.

74 FRANK 'CANNONBALL' RICHARD

– The Punching Bag

The pain proof man has existed in one form or another for centuries. From fakirs walking on hot coals, to persons of extraordinary physiology like the great Mirin Dajo, to persons driving nails deep into their various facial orifices. However, few individuals have captured the imagination of the modern pop culture audience than the amazing Frank 'Cannonball' Richards.

In 1932, 'Cannonball' Richards exploded onto the vaudeville entertainment scene with his remarkable act and his bombastic belly. Frank's claim to fame was his seemingly ironclad gut and his act consisted of little more than taking heavy blows to his belly.

However, these were no gentle taps. Richards subjected his belly to physical abuse that would put an average man into hospitalised traction for days – if not weeks.

Richards began his strange journey into belly abuse by allowing his friends to punch him in the gut. His perceived imperviousness to the

trauma prompted him to take the act a step further until, eventually, he was enduring and absorbing body blows from heavyweight boxing champion Jack Dempsey.

'Cannonball' Richards steadily increased the level of distress he subjected his belly to. He soon allowed spectators to jump on his stomach. Following that, he allowed himself to be struck by a two-by-four and then, later he was able to endure repeated sledgehammer blows. From all reports and records, there were no gimmicks at work during these performances.

Finally, in a feat that 'Cannonball' Richards would forever be remembered for, Richards took to being shot in the belly with a cannonball.

It is important to note that 'Cannonball' Richards used a spring-loaded cannon to fire his cannonball. But equally, the velocity at which the ball travelled was still beyond the limits of sanity and would likely have killed or severely injured an average man.

The image of this feat, performed twice daily during his time of greatest popularity, remains a near iconic photograph demonstrating the extremes possible in physical pain tolerance. It is also regarded, incorrectly, the epitome of stupidity and ultimate example of a fame without talent or ability. So much so that during the seventh season, in an episode of *The Simpsons* animated television series the idiotic and chronically talentless Homer Simpson was hired into a travelling freak show, to be shot by cannonballs in the stomach.

It is a shame that most modern audiences have not realised the dedication and daredevil spirit required to perform the stunts Richards performed. So unique was his ability that no comparable act has existed since.

LE PETOMANE

– The Fartiste

Born in Marseilles, France in 1857, Joseph Pujol eventually became one of the most unique performers ever to grace a stage.

Legend has is that one day, while swimming, Pujol discovered his unique ability. As he took a deep breath before submerging, he felt water enter his rear. He soon discovered that with abdominal control, he could deliberately suck water in through his anus and project it back out with great force. Further experimentation led him to discover that he could also do the same with air and by varying pressures, he could produce distinct notes.

Pujol became the first flatulence musician. It was a skill that eventually made him the most well-known and highest paid entertainer in all of France.

Billed as 'Le Pétomane', Pujol began his career as a comedy act in 1887 at the age of 30. However, encouraged by success in his native Marseilles, Pujol began to take his ability seriously and within five years he was headlining the Moulin Rouge in Paris.

On stage, dressed in a fine red coat and black britches, Le Pétomane began each performance by explaining to his audience that his emissions were odourless. After reassuring the masses, he would launch into his act. He would start with a comedy series of what he called 'fart impressions'. He would emit a tiny toot, label it as the fart of a 'new bride', then flap a thunderous emission and label it as the same bride a week into the marriage. He did impressions of famous people, squeezed out a ten-second long squeaker, and then blew out candles using nothing but by the gases emitted from his posterior.

For his finale, Le Pétomane inserted a rubber tube into his anus, attached an ocarina to the end of the hose, and played popular tunes while inviting the audience to sing along.

He was a great success at the Moulin Rouge and eventually opened his own theatre where he continued to perform until his popularity waned during WWI. He retired from show business in 1914 and in 1945 Joseph Pujol passed away at the age of eighty-eight.

Following his death, medical schools in Paris clamoured to examine the late Le Pétomane's famous anus. The family declined all inquiries stating that there are some things in this life which simply must be treated with reverence.

MIRIN DAJO

– The Extreme Human Pincushion

The man in the picture is Dutch fakir Mirin Dajo. He was born in 1912 as Arnold Gerrit Henskes and adopted his name, an Esperanto term that translates to mean 'wonderful'. In 1947, at the Corso Theatre in Zurich, Mirin Dajo allowed an assistant to plunge a fencing foil right through his body. The foil appeared to have pierced several vital organs and yet, the fakir remained relatively unharmed. Needless to say, people were shocked, amazed and terrified by what they saw.

As word of his remarkable talent spread, a Swiss doctor Hans Naegeli-Osjord invited Mirin Dajo to the Zurich Cantonal hospital for study. Many people, including Naegeli-Osjord, the chief of surgery Dr. Werner Brunnerand as well as several other doctors, students and members of the press witnessed these tests. All were dumbfounded by what they saw.

In front of the witnesses assembled, Mirin Dajo stripped naked to the waist and following a period of meditation, once again had his assistant plunge the steel rapier through him. He then stood for some time, impaled, while the doctors examined him.

The doctors could find no evidence of trickery but many still refused to believe what they saw. Mirin Dajo agreed to an x-ray with the foil in place. The resulting image confirmed the legitimacy of his abilities.

Later that same year, Mirin Dajo was again submitted to examination , this time in Basel. There he actually allowed the doctors themselves to pierce him. Again, there was no evidence of trickery. Not only did Mirin Dajo insist the doctors to treat him roughly, he later jogged several laps while still impaled to illustrate his complete tolerance of pain.

Mirin Dajo was a very religious man and some media outlets labelled him a 'Messiah'. According to some reports, Mirin Dajo could hear voices, a spiritual guide. His public displays were often concluded with a lecture and a message of peace.

He kept performing his feat for audiences. Eventually, to prove his talent was real while on stage, he took to being impaled by three hollow skewers. He would then pump water through those skewers. He became a human fountain.

It is not uncommon for eastern fakirs to pierce themselves with swords, many of them can push swords completely through their bodies. However, the majority of them do so through the fatty and safe areas their body. The piercing feats of Mirin Dajo were extreme.

It is important to note that his unique skill may have resulted in his demise on May 26, 1948. An autopsy revealed that Dajo died of an aortic rupture.

77 MARTIN LAURELLO

– The Human Owl

The gentleman depicted is Martin Laurello, born Martin Emmerling, and he hailed from Nuremburg, Germany. He was an anatomical wonder, able to turn his head 180 degrees. How he accomplished this feat is unknown.

Martin first appeared in the United States in 1921 though he had performed in Europe previously. Initially, he was tied to Dreamland circus but he also did stints with Barnum & Bailey, Ringling Bros. and, perhaps most notably, with Ripley's Odditorium. His last recorded appearance was in 1945, with Ripley.

It was rumoured that Martin was a Nazi sympathiser. His attitude did little to endear him to his fellow performers. It is likely that Martin burnt too many bridges in the sideshow community and opted to retire. No one knows what became of him, but it is rumoured that he passed away in the 1950's.

78 DOMINIQUE CASTAGNA

– The Mummy

The Living Skeleton was a fairly common human marvel appearing in private exhibits and travelling sideshows during the heyday of human exhibition. Living Skeletons, sometimes referred to as 'shadows', were generally adult men afflicted with some sort of consumption disease ranging from digestive disorders to full blown cases of tuberculosis. Living Skeletons were emaciated to a startling degree, many of them weighed less than 75 pounds and some weighed as little as 50 pounds.

The Living Skeleton was often presented in tandem with a Fat Lady to better juxtapose the physical attributes of both. In fact, it was a common practice amongst showmen to stage a wedding ceremony between a Fat Lady and a Living Skeleton to capitalise on free publicity and draw crowds.

The list of Living Skeletons is long, but few were as unfortunate as Dominique Castagna – The Mummy.

Born in Slaligny, France in 1869, Dominique Castagna was, by all accounts, an ugly child. His face was contorted, his eyes were buggy and his nose was compressed and flat. To make matters worse, at the age of two he stopped developing normally. His appearance quickly became gaunt and emaciated and his growth stunted. By the age of twelve, he was fully grown and as an adult he was only 4' 9" and weighed only 50 pounds and 6 ounces. Due to his appearance, Castagna was extremely introvert and lonely. He had few friends and was generally avoided by all who saw him as he was assumed to be deathly ill and contagious.

Initially, Dominique Castagna tried to live a normal life, but his frail body and looks didn't allow for a great range of career choices. While working as an office assistant for an architect in Monaco, a co-worker named Cruzel convinced him to exhibit himself for profit. Dominique Castagna reasoned that, since he was always stared at anyway, he may as well make some money in the process. Still, he was greatly reluctant to be made a spectacle. It was with great trepidation that he entered show business.

Castagna exhibited himself in Marseille for the first time in 1896. Cruzel acted as his agent during that venture and every venture afterward. It was Cruzel who dubbed Castagna – The Mummy, inspired by the sunken features and boney body of Castagna. The name stuck and, perhaps despite the label, Cruzel and Castagna became great friends.

Castagna was overjoyed to be accepted by someone who, over time, no longer saw the disfigurements and physical peculiarities. Cruzel accepted Castagna as he was and with his friendship Castagna was able to ignore the more miserable aspects of his life. He hated exhibition and the constant stares. He was torn apart by his loneliness and the lack of love in his life.

When his friend Cruzel married and quit show business, Castagna shot himself in a hotel in Leige in 1905.

79 ISAAC W. SPRAGUE

– The Original Living Skeleton

Isaac W. Sprague was born on May 21, 1841 in East Bridgewater, Massachusetts. According to one of his early cabinet cards, he was a normal and active child until the age of twelve – when he began to rapidly lose weight.

His concerned parents, alarmed by his weight lost, forbade young Isaac from high energy activities. Despite this, the boy continued to loose weight and his terrified parents took Isaac to the best doctors they could find. Unfortunately, the doctors were also baffled and Isaac continued to wither away despite a healthy appetite.

As an adult, Isaac apprenticed under his father as a cobbler and later worked as a grocer. However, as his emaciation continued, Isaac found his energy depleted. It soon became too difficult for Isaac to continue working – it was then that the world of sideshow came calling.

In 1865, during a visit to a local carnival, a promoter spotted Isaac and offered him a job. At first, the young man refused. But he soon realised that he could earn a good living by capitalising on his looks. He began touring as 'The Living Skeleton' and quickly rose in popularity. In less than a year, he auditioned for P. T. Barnum and was hired on a salary of $80 a week.

His career with Barnum was brief as Barnum's American Museum burned down for the second time in 1868. Isaac barely managed to escape the museum alive – following his escape, he left sideshow for a while.

During his premature retirement, he met and married a Miss Tamar Moore and had three healthy sons. In dire straights due to poor financial decisions, he resumed touring with Barnum and others. His financial problems, and perhaps a gambling addiction resulted in Isaac W. Sprague dying in poverty on January 5, 1887 in Chicago.

While his weight varied over his career, an official measurement was taken by a physician when Isaac was forty-four. At a height of five feet and six inches, Isaac weighed only forty-three pounds.

Despite numerous medical exams during his lifetime, his condition was never officially identified. He was labelled as having 'an extreme case of progressive muscular atrophy'. As a result Isaac was required to eat constantly. In fact, he was well-known to carry a flask of sweetened dairy milk around his neck which he drank from time to time to keep himself alive and conscious.

Believe it or not, the 'Living Skeleton' came to be a fairly common sideshow attraction. In fact, it was not uncommon, in a feat of inspired promotion, for a sideshow Skeleton Man to marry the local Fat Lady in an extravagant ceremony. The local press was, of course, always invited to attend.

JAMES MORRIS

– The Rubber Man

James Morris was born in Copenhagen New York in 1859 and used his unique talent to amuse friends and coworkers from a young age. His ability to stretch his skin as much as eighteen inches from his body, with no perceivable pain made him incredibly popular with officers when he joined the military. Those officers invited reporters and journalists to witness Morris's unusual talent and from there Morris was recruited by several circuses, sideshow and dime museums. By 1885, he travelled the world and joined up with the Barnum and Bailey Circus.

With Barnum and Bailey, he was exhibited throughout North America and Europe and in 1898 he was featured in Scientific America as 'The Rubber Man'. For the journal, he pulled the skin of his neck over his head to which it was reported to resemble 'an elephant's trunk'.

As detailed in an earlier post, 'Rubber Men' were afflicted with a condition known as cutis hyperelastica or Ehlers-Danlos Syndrome. The syndrome results in a defect in collagen synthesis which in turn results in overly stretchable, and elastic, fragile, soft skin that easily forms welts and scars.

While Morris earned good money in his first season with Barnum and Bailey, his popularity quickly dwindled due to a slight drinking and gambling problem, he took a second job as a barber opening a shop in New York City.

81 ROBERT MELVIN

– The Man with Two Faces

The moniker 'The Man with Two Faces' has been given to many marvels during the history of sideshow. While few actually had two faces, Robert Melvin came pretty close. Born in Missouri on May 9, 1920 as one of the six children, it quickly became evident that Robert was different. He was examined quite extensively by doctors during his childhood and yet his condition remained undiagnosed for many years. It wasn't until later in life that Robert was finally diagnosed with neurofibromatosis; a disorder that causes the spontaneous growth of fibrous tumors.

Neurofibromatosis, or NF as it is commonly referred to, is quite varied in its visible symptoms. Some patients are greatly deformed, some have small nodules or knots on their bodies, and some have little more than a few small brown birthmarks. There has been great speculation that Joseph Merrick – The Elephant Man, had NF. One look at the facial deformities Robert possessed and their similarity to those of The Elephant Man gives some merit to those assumptions; although, it is still mere speculation. For a time, Robert was even known as 'The Modern Elephant Man'. Many people were so shocked at Robert's appearance that many believed he was a fake – even a few noted doctors and sideshow historians.

The tumors that afflicted Robert completely distorted the features on the right side of his face. While Robert was not allowed to attend school as a child due to his appearance, he did receive a full education. And through the power of his unbelievably outgoing personality, he became rather well-known, respected and loved by his small town neighbours. He never considered his appearance a handicap. In fact, once he entered the world of sideshow in 1949 at Coney Island, his appearance became a great advantage.

Robert made a comfortable living with the sideshow both as an attraction and serving as the show accountant. During the off season, Robert kept busy doing the books for a hardware store. He also enjoyed a minor film career, appearing as a sanitarium inmate in *Sisters* (1973) along with fellow marvel Bill Durks as a surreal demon in *The Sentinel* (1977) and also in the documentaries *Being Different* (1981) and *I Am Not a Freak* (1987).

In 1952, Robert returned to his hometown and married his longtime girlfriend Virginia a girl he had known since his mid teenaged years and despite rumours that 'it would never last' the pair were married for more than forty years. The two had a daughter, who later gave Robert a grandson and granddaughter.

Robert was known by friends and family – including the extended family he met in the sideshow – as a friendly, gentle, charming and intelligent man. When he passed away on November 19 in 1995, his funeral was well attended by those who loved and respected 'The Man with Two Faces' for the marvelous man that he was.